ROBERT BARNARD

Award-winning author of *A City of Strangers*

DEATH OF A SALESPERSON:
AND OTHER UNTIMELY EXITS

"SIXTEEN BEASTLY BEAUTIES, EACH BARING SHARP TEETH BEHIND A MALICIOUS GRIN."
—*The New York Times Book Review*

N 0-440-20587-5>>395

9 780440 205876

50395

**Don't Miss These
Irresistible Mysteries from Dell by**

ROBERT BARNARD

DEATH AND THE CHASTE
 APPRENTICE
AT DEATH'S DOOR
THE SKELETON IN THE GRASS
THE CHERRY BLOSSOM CORPSE
BODIES
POLITICAL SUICIDE
FÊTE FATALE
OUT OF THE BLACKOUT
CORPSE IN A GILDED CAGE
SCHOOL FOR MURDER
THE CASE OF THE MISSING BRONTË
A LITTLE LOCAL MURDER
DEATH AND THE PRINCESS
DEATH BY SHEER TORTURE
DEATH IN A COLD CLIMATE
DEATH OF A PERFECT MOTHER
DEATH OF A LITERARY WIDOW
DEATH OF A MYSTERY WRITER
DEATH ON THE HIGH C's

ROBERT BARNARD
Death of a Salesperson
and Other Untimely Exits

BY THE SAME AUTHOR

Death
of a
Salesperson

and Other Untimely Exits

ROBERT BARNARD

A DELL BOOK

Published by
Dell Publishing
a division of
Bantam Doubleday Dell Publishing Group, Inc.
666 Fifth Avenue
New York, New York 10103

ISBN: 0-440-20587-5

Reprinted by arrangement with Macmillan Publishing
Company.

Printed in the United States of America

February 1991

10   9   8   7   6   5   4   3   2   1

OPM

CONTENTS

Death
of a
Salesperson

THE WOMAN IN THE WARDROBE

It was after the funeral, when the relatives and friends had gone and the house felt cold and empty, that Geoffrey Harcourt felt his loss most keenly. The beginning of my aloneness, he thought. It was Monday, too, the start of the school's half-term holiday. Of course he could go along to the office: there was always work for a headmaster to do. But that would only be exchanging one emptiness for another. There were friends he could visit, but he knew that their avoidance of him was partly from the kindliest of motives, partly to spare themselves awkwardness. Geoffrey was a reticent man, not one to hawk around his sense of loss.

The vicar had told him how it would be, and he had been right. In fact, the vicar phoned him that evening, knowing how low he would feel after the funeral. Geoffrey had been listening to Mahler. He had always said that Mahler was getting to be that bit overrated, but in his current state the Ninth said things to him that it had never said before. The things they said were not comfortable things, though. He got more comfort from his chat with the vicar.

'Try to keep busy,' the vicar said in his normal voice, which was a comfort after all the hushed tones. 'There must be lots of books around the house that were Helen's rather than yours. The library would probably be grateful for them. Good second-hand clothes are always in demand, particularly in hard times like the present. We at the church could get rid of them for you. I don't mean that you should wipe the house clean of all reminders of her—heaven forbid! But you'll be glad in a month or two's time that you don't have those things still to do . . . You're not brooding on this man, are you? The driver?'

'No,' said Geoffrey truthfully. 'There doesn't seem much point. I'd like to see him caught and banned from driving for life, but beyond that . . . We don't even know it was a man, by the way . . . We don't even *know* it was a Honda. That was just the witness's impression—a silver-blue Honda . . . No, I'm truly not brooding over him. It's just the emptiness.'

'I know, old chap. As I say, just try to keep busy. I'll come round in a few days and see if you've got anything for us.'

So for the rest of the evening Geoffrey combed through the various bookcases that dotted the house. He found twenty or thirty books—novels, travel books, books connected with the sociology course that Helen had been doing at the City Polytechnic. He made them up into a rough parcel, and told himself he would ring the library next day. Certainly the activity had kept his mind occupied.

In the morning, after breakfast—the time of day when he and Helen had been most entirely together—he decided to tackle the clothes. Really he could not see that he need keep anything at all. He shrank from asking any of his or Helen's relatives if they would like anything, and he was quite certain they would in any case refuse. Helen's interest in clothes was strictly utilitarian: she bought what would wear well, what was suitable for a headmaster's wife. There was no sentimental feeling involved. His mind was crowded with memories of Helen, but what she had worn on those occasions he would have been quite at a loss to say.

He put two old suitcases on the bed and opened the half of the wardrobe that contained the drawers. He piled underclothes and nightgowns, tights and hats into one case —and though he did it quickly and expertly he was surprised to find when he had finished that he was nearly crying. Should he make himself a cup of coffee? No. He would finish first. Ten minutes would do it easily.

He threw open the other door. His first emotion was

merely a dim kind of puzzlement: something was not quite right. It was only after a few seconds that the full impact hit him. Here were all the clothes that he—absent-mindedly —knew so well: dresses, suits she had worn to school functions, the three-quarter length gown she wore to their very occasional dinner-dance. But here too . . . He went forward and fingered them wonderingly.

In the darkest, innermost part of the wardrobe were clothes he had never seen. Clothes he could never imagine Helen wearing. They were bright, sensuous clothes, in rich materials—silks, cashmeres. He kept feeling them, as if that would make them real. He could not take his bewildered eyes off them. These were the clothes of a woman of the world: smart, fashionable clothes. He had seen women dressed like this in Bond Street; he could imagine the woman who owned them in the stalls at Covent Garden, dancing at the Dorchester. That evening dress—it shimmered; it was positively glamorous.

He shut the wardrobe door sharply, and leaned his head against it for a moment. Then he went downstairs to make that cup of coffee. He sat down at the kitchen table to drink it, and tried to collect his thoughts.

He rejected almost as soon as it entered his head the idea that she was storing the clothes for a friend. What friend had she that would wear clothes like *that*? Why would she be asked to store only the expensive, fashionable clothes? No, they were Helen's. She had known that, short of her being very ill, he would never think of looking in her wardrobe. What did she want them for? Did she wear them during the day while he was at school? Did she float around the house in a dream of aristocratic elegance, imagining herself at cocktails in Mayfair, dancing the night away at some aristocratic sprig's twenty-first? It seemed so unlike Helen. His wife had been a competent, down-to-earth, no-nonsense woman. So he had always believed.

He steeled himself to go back to the bedroom. He took

the clothes from the wardrobe, ran his hand over their softness, felt their textures, admired their cut. He was no expert, had always had to remind himself to comment on his wife's appearance if they were going out, but these clothes seemed to him immensely stylish: they were the sort of clothes worn by women who were rich, confident and attractive. Helen had inherited a house in suburban London when her mother died, and had sold it at the current inflated prices. The problem was not where she had got the money from. It was why she had felt the desire.

That afternoon he rang the City Polytechnic. He got on to the Admissions Secretary at once.

'Hello. My name is Geoffrey Harcourt. I'm ringing about my wife, Helen Harcourt.'

'Oh yes, I remember her well,' said a friendly female voice. 'We had many good chats when she was deciding on her course.'

'I think she told me about them. I'm afraid she's dead.'

'Oh dear. I *am* sorry. Had she been ill for some time?'

'It was a road accident. A hit-and-run driver.'

'How *awful*. It must have been a terrible shock for you.'

'It was. I just thought I'd ring to inform you, so you can take her off your books.'

There was a pause of fully three seconds before the woman said: 'Yes, of course, we'll do that. And once again, I *am* sorry.'

Geoffrey knew what that pause meant, knew what the woman had been about to say, and had stopped herself from saying: Helen had not been on their books for some time.

His night was awful. He lay on the double bed they had shared, feet away from the wardrobe. Nightmarishly it seemed to him that in the wardrobe he had discovered another woman, a woman who was his wife and was not his wife. Helen had had another life unknown to him, in which she was glamorous, fashionable, even seductive. It was as if some sudden crisis or involuntary action had revealed to him a side to his own nature of which he had always been unconscious. Helen was not *like* that, he kept saying to himself, had no desire for that kind of life. She was, she had, said the wardrobe.

By next morning he knew he could not leave things there: he had to *know*. He had a grey, old-fashioned Puritan conscience. What his discovery was whispering to him was that somehow he had failed Helen. Still more that meant he had to *know*.

Over breakfast, feeling furtive and grubby, he went through Helen's cheque-book and the monthly statements of her credit card company. So far as he could see there were no hotel bills. When Helen had started staying overnight on Thursdays ('There are so many evening activities that I'm missing out on, and British Rail has practically cut out all the trains after nine') she had told him she had found a little bed-and-breakfast place in Bloomsbury that was clean and cheap. There were no cheque-stubs to bear this out. Nor were there cheques made out to more glamorous hotels. There were, though, largish sums on the statement: they were paid to Harrods, Selfridges, and a shop called Amanda's, which was in Knightsbridge. The clothes, obviously.

His mind honed in on the sociology course. They had discussed it quite a bit at first, hardly at all recently. The subjects had become too esoteric, and besides Geoffrey had the natural contempt of the academic mind for such a subject. It had been a one-day-a-week course, aimed at part-time students and people with special needs. When she had started she had gone on Wednesdays. Some way into the first year she had said that the day had been changed to Thursdays. But wouldn't that have been immensely disruptive of the students' arrangements, and wouldn't the timetable readjustments have been difficult or impossible? She had changed to Thursdays because . . . But no. Best to put any such thoughts aside. Stick to facts. Keep a firm grip

on reality. He had to look at the newspaper to establish that
the day was in fact Wednesday.

He took the car up to London. He couldn't face the
sympathy and inquiries of the people at the station. At
Carbury, the small Essex town where he lived, everyone
knew everyone. He drove to the City Polytechnic, then
round and round it for twenty minutes until he saw a car
pulling out. He nosed into the parking space, and walked
into the Poly. In the foyer he prowled around until he found
the notice-board with the timetables. With his practised
headmaster's eye he skimmed over the mass of detailed
information (so many courses, so little knowledge) till he
came to 'Sociology (Special Needs)'. If Helen had continued
she would now be taking—had said she *was* taking—the
third-year course.

He was right. The course was on Wednesdays. The group
was currently engaged in a seminar on The Battered Child
Syndrome in room 347B. They would be out at twelve
o'clock. He took the lift up to the third floor, and walked
through the tedious, anonymous corridors. More like a
business firm or a rather run-down hotel than a place of
education, he thought. How had Helen fitted in here? Had
she ever felt at home? He stationed himself near 347B,
feeling like a novice plain-clothes policeman.

When the seminar broke up the students trailed out
looking bored. It was difficult to imagine how a terrible,
touching subject like battered children could be made boring, but the lecturer seemed to have managed it somehow.
About a third of the students were the normal college-age
young, others were in their twenties or thirties, the rest
Helen's age or older. He picked out a sympathetic woman
of about forty and went hesitantly up to her.

'Excuse me, I wonder if you can help me. I'm looking for
someone who knew Helen Harcourt when she was a student
here.'

The woman turned and smiled.

'Oh yes, I knew Helen.'

'Well?'

'As well as anyone here, I suppose. Those of us who'd reached the forties mark tended to get together between classes. Why?'

'I'm her husband. Helen died in a road accident last week.'

'Oh *dear*. How tragic. She was so gay and vital.'

'Look, would you let me buy you lunch? Is there anywhere around here?'

'I'll let you buy me lunch, but in the canteen. It's not too bad. I don't know what you want of me, but it can't be worth the price of a restaurant meal.'

Over two plates of shepherd's pie and peas Geoffrey put his cards on the table.

'Since my wife died I've discovered things about her that I never knew before. I didn't know she had given up her course here, for example, and there are ... other things. She had a life, for one day a week, of which I knew nothing. Please believe it's not anger or pique that makes me feel I have to know. You won't be betraying Helen in anything you tell me. I just want to find out how I failed her.'

The woman nodded.

'I can understand that. But truly I know nothing that could "betray" her in any way. We weren't that kind of friends, and she was only here for a term and a half, you know.'

'That's what I guessed. Why did she give it up? She seemed so enthusiastic at first.'

'Oh, she was. We all were. But the teaching is not too good, and some of the subject areas seem just plain potty. I remember Helen once said to me that she wondered whether it *was* a subject at all ... In fact, quite a lot of us wonder why we go on. Just to get a bit of paper at the end, I suppose.'

'And that was the reason she stopped?'

'I don't know the reason she stopped. But she was expressing boredom, and then one week she wasn't there. She never came again.'

'I see. Tell me, did she have any special friends?'

'Well, we're all quite good friends. The young ones tend to keep to themselves, but they're really quite *kind* to us . . . I see what you're getting at, of course . . . There was a man . . . Oh dear, what was his name? There was a Polytechnic party and dance, early in second term that year . . .'

'Yes, I seem to remember. Helen took the car and drove back very late. I was asleep when she got back in.'

'I'm sure it meant nothing special, but she danced a lot with this man. He gave up the course about the time she did, I think, which is why I can't remember his name. He was five or six years younger than Helen, but they seemed to find each other a lot of fun. His business had collapsed, but he was hoping for a job with ICI on the personnel side. This course was a sort of stop-gap. As far as I remember, he got the job and stopped coming.'

'There's nothing else you can remember about him—about them—that might suggest—'

'That they were having an affair? That is what we're talking about, isn't it? Oh dear, I *do* feel this is a betrayal . . . To an outsider it seemed so much more, at that stage, a matter of a shared sense of humour than an affair. I remember once, when we were all sitting talking in here, this man gave us a marvellous account, with miming and accents and all, of this hotel in Bloomsbury—the Durward, that was it —where they still do real old-fashioned teas, with dainty sandwiches and tea-cake and muffins. And they have dancing after dinner with a Palm Court Orchestra, and lots of faded elegance. I remember your wife laughing till she ached, and saying: "Just like *Bertram's Hotel*. I'd love to see it." And this man promised to take her one day . . . What *was* his name?'

'Would anybody else remember?'

'They might do.' She looked around and darted to a table with three or four older students. 'His name was Roger Michaels,' she said when she returned. 'He'd owned a small toy factory, but the recession had closed it. And it was ICI he went to.' She leaned forward very earnestly. 'You do realize I've no *evidence*—'

'Oh, of course. It could be someone else entirely—someone she met on the train, for instance. It could be no one. By the way, what did he look like?'

'Dapper. Well set up, but not tall. Lively, always darting here and there. Lots and lots of jokes.'

I've never been good on jokes, thought Geoffrey sadly. It seemed as though some great weight was pressing on his back, squeezing the breath out of him. How I failed her, he thought. He had known his wife had been kind, generous, considerate. Now he also knew she had craved colour, gaiety, laughter. How totally he had failed her.

It was still early afternoon when he got back to his car. He rather thought he had enough information to track down this Roger Michaels, but first there was something else he could try, to see if he was on the right scent. Helen's friend had been right when she said what they were talking about was an affair. The clothes were the clothes of a woman in love. But was Michaels the man? He drove to Bloomsbury, and once again drove round and round before he found a parking space. Then he marked time in Dillons and Foyles until it was four o'clock, and tea would be served at the Durward.

It was overpoweringly genteel, like Harrogate in the 'thirties. A pianist played Gershwin and Ivor Novello, quite softly, and the sandwiches and cakes nestled in lacy doylies on silver baskets. Only the staff were wrong: a heterogeneous collection of nationalities. Geoffrey was lucky: he had a genial, pot-bellied Cypriot with an East London accent. When he was half way through his tea he fished from his wallet the photograph of Helen, taken on holiday the year before in Verona, and beckoned the waiter over. His first reaction was to shake his head.

'No. No, I can't say I have . . . Wait! Wait a minute, though. I think that must be Mrs Rogers, so called. Yes— I'd bet my bottom . . . Mind you, she looks so different there. Quite dowdy, really, as if she'd tried to de-glamourize herself. Our Mrs Rogers . . . What is this all about, mate? Private detective, are you? I suppose it'll be the real Mrs Rogers, or whatever her name is.'

'When are you off?'

'I finish at six, thank Gawd.'

'Care for a drink?'

'I wouldn't say no.'

'Meet you outside at six.'

Settled into the Jug and Bottle, just off the Tottenham Court Road, and after a tenner had passed between them, the waiter told Geoffrey all he knew.

'Somehow I always had the suspicion they weren't married. I saw him sign the register when they first stayed the night here, and he didn't do it confident-like. What ho! I thought. Your name isn't Michael Rogers. Since then I've noticed he always pays cash, never cheque or credit card.'

'But they register as husband and wife?'

''Course they do. What do you think? Mind you, it is a bit out of the usual run of liaisons. Because when you look close you realize she is older than him. Glamorous, very smart, altogether the superior article, but older. I put her down as a lady from the provinces—and I do *mean* a lady, and a well-heeled one—'aving a fling in London. Though it's more than that, too. You can see she is in love.'

The waiter, drinking deep, did not see Geoffrey flinch.

'Do they come to the Durward every week?'

'Oh yes, they have been doing. 'Cept in the holidays. I put it down to one or other of them having kiddies home from boarding-school.'

'So they come every Thursday?'

'That's right. Not last week, but it's probably half term or something. Yes, they come down and have tea in the Garden Room, same as you just done.'

'What do they do in the evenings?'

'Sometimes they have dinner at the Durward, and a dance afterwards. But Thursday nights is not very lively. Mostly they go out. Taxi called from the desk, then off to the Savoy or wherever. She in long dress, hair done, beautifully made-up. My God, she can look a stunner! I don't wonder he was taken.'

'You said that she's in love. Is he?'

'Oh, I think so. Not a doubt of it. At least until recently . . .'

'There has been a change?'

'Well, there has and there hasn't. On the surface everything has been the same. But they've got more serious. Had long conversations in low voices over the tea-table. Once I could see she was distressed—though *being* a lady, she was always the same to me if I came up to see if there was anything they wanted . . . He wasn't upset in quite that way, and I put the change down to him trying to wind up the affair—in the nicest possible way. Say what you like, that's what usually happens when the woman's the older one. Mind you, thinking back on it, he could have been telling her that his wife was suspicious, and they'd have to go careful for a bit.'

No, Geoffrey thought; he'd used her, and was giving her the brush-off. He was conceiving an intense dislike for this Roger Michaels, who worked for ICI and had this great store of jokes. What he felt—he told himself with the bleak honesty of someone whose emotional voltage was low—was not jealousy. Or not primarily jealousy. It was indignation on Helen's behalf. He saw her now as someone who had for years modified her personality to suit the grey, even life which her marriage had offered her, but who had had that other, more daring self waiting to spring out. And when it had done, she had been used by a thoughtless or heartless man, and then thrown aside.

'I feel guilty about this,' said the waiter, standing up and patting his back pocket, 'but a tenner's a tenner. I don't know what the lady who's paying you is like, but *my* pair are nice people. And *she* is a beautiful woman.'

I never knew I was married to a beautiful woman, thought Geoffrey sadly.

Next morning the great weight of failure, of lack of understanding, seemed as crushing as ever. Before breakfast he drove to his school. It was like a ghost school, though later, he knew, one of the secretaries would be coming in. He took the L to R volume of the London Telephone Directory from the office and drove home. He spoke to nobody. Still less, now, did he wish to have a heart-to-heart with anyone about his loss.

Michaels, fortunately, was not a common name. With the data he had on him Geoffrey could make a guess at the sort of area he might live in, and from the handful who had the initial R he struck gold with his second call. It was to the R. Michaels who lived in Grafton Avenue, Surbiton.

'Could I speak to Mr Michaels, please?'

'I'm afraid my husband is away at his job from Mondays to Fridays. Can I help?'

It was a hard, tight little voice, quite neutral in accent.

'Perhaps you can. I'm with the *Economist*, and we're doing a survey of British toy manufacturers—'

'Oh, my husband got out of that long ago. Nearly two years. He saw the way the wind was blowing. He's got a very good job with ICI now.'

'Thank you. That tells me what I want to know. I shan't need to trouble you again.'

On an impulse, when he had put the phone down, he looked up the number for ICI and got on to the personnel department.

'I'm sorry, but Mr Michaels isn't here at the moment,' a

cool, competent voice told him. 'His main work is with our businesses in the North. He drives up there on Monday mornings, and he only comes in here on Fridays, though I believe he drives down on Thursday afternoon.'

When he had put the phone down, Geoffrey began wondering about Roger Michaels's arrangements with Helen. Did they meet somewhere, then go on to the Durward together? That seemed likely. Had he been expecting to meet her last Thursday, and would he be waiting again today? Or had he, as the waiter conjectured, broken it off —disguising it, perhaps, as a temporary break while his wife was suspicious, but in brutal reality ditching her?

By now he had made up his mind: at some time in the future he was going to have to have a talk with Roger Michaels.

But first he wanted to suss out the lie of the land, sniff out the character of his everyday life. He found Grafton Avenue easily in his *London A–Z*. There was nothing to prevent him driving there at once. Half term had still some days to run, and doubtless any problems that came up were referred to the Deputy Head. When he got to Surbiton he found that at least here parking was no problem. There didn't seem to be much else to be said for the place. He put the car in the next street and walked casually along Grafton Avenue. The Michaels's house was not very different from what he had expected: a standard detached house, probably built in the 'fifties, with a tiny, neat front garden, and no character whatsoever. The same was true of all the houses in the street: suburbia personified. The only relief from the architectural monotony was a small square of public garden on the opposite corner of the avenue. Geoffrey walked in it for a bit, his eye on Roger's house, but there was no sign of life.

Was Roger a pub man, he wondered? Yes, it did sound as if Roger was probably a pub man. Men with streams of jokes usually were. Two streets away Geoffrey could see the outlines of a 'thirties roadhouse, brewery-anonymous in style. Could that be Roger Michaels's local? It seemed worth a try.

It was still a good half-hour before the lunch-time rush, and the landlord was ready for a leisurely gossip.

Thinking of moving round here, was he? Well, he always did say you couldn't find a nicer area. Lovely houses—well, he would have seen that. Nice people too, if it came to that —a very good *class*, if Geoffrey knew what he meant. What line of business was Geoffrey in himself? Schoolmastering? *Head*master! Well, he could practically guarantee he would fit in perfectly. Did he have any connections in this area?

'Oh no,' said Geoffrey airily. 'Not really. Though I've just remembered I do know a chap who lives around here somewhere. Man called Roger Michaels.'

'Roger! One of the best. He's one of our regulars—well, not regular, because these days he's up North from Monday to Friday. But he'll be in on Friday or Saturday, and he and his wife come in at Sunday lunch-time without fail. Come in about half past twelve, have a couple, then leave about half past one, when the roast is done.'

'Great chap, Roger,' said Geoffrey, with painfully assumed heartiness.

'Lovely man. Really funny. I'd say he was a real wit. He gets a little circle round him when he comes in here, and he has them splitting their sides.'

'Bit of a lad too, I believe,' said Geoffrey.

'Oh, we wouldn't know about that round here,' said the landlord with professional caution. 'While he's home his wife keeps him on a very tight leash. Between you and me—' he leant forward over the bar, and hushed his voice— 'she has the reputation of being a bit of a b.i.t.c.h. . . . Mind you, if he has his fling now and then, I'm not alto*gethe*r surprised.'

'No?'

The landlord lowered his voice again.

'Couple round here had their Silver Wedding. Went to

the Savoy for a bit of a splash. They saw Roger there with a woman—a real corker, so they said. 'Course, it could have been his sister . . .' The landlord smirked. 'Nothing was said. Just one or two dirty snickers. The fact is, his lady wife's not greatly liked. And you can say what you want about Roger, he's a man people take to.'

Then the bar began to fill up.

Geoffrey went back to the roadhouse on Sunday at lunchtime. The bar was full this time, and he was served by a barmaid. He stationed himself by the window. From here he could not see the Michaels's house, but he could see the end of Grafton Avenue. Most of the couples who came for a drink drove, but surely the Michaelses would not. At about half past midday he saw a couple walking from Grafton Avenue. They were apparently affectionate, but there was something forced about it, even from a distance. He walked like a man with something on his mind. She took his hand in hers, but that only increased the sense of strain. As they approached the pub Geoffrey downed his drink and escaped out the back. In the car he found he was drenched with sweat.

That, certainly, had not been the time or the place for an encounter. He had to get Michaels on his own, in some place where neither of them was known. But how could that be arranged?

On Sunday night Geoffrey rang his Deputy Head. He found he just couldn't face school in the morning, he said. He'd intended coming in, but somehow the thought of school assembly, with all the children looking at him, was more than he could bear. He might slip in inconspicuously later in the day, or he'd be there without fail on Tuesday. His Deputy was very sympathetic, and said she quite understood.

It was very dark when Geoffrey left the house on Monday morning—still night, in fact. Roger Michaels's time of departure for the North could be anything from six onwards.

In fact Geoffrey was in position in the little patch of public garden by five past. He had left his car just round the corner from Grafton Avenue. At about twenty past a light came on in the landing of No. 26, and soon there seemed to be lights on in the back of the house downstairs. What was he doing? Making himself coffee, or making himself breakfast? Geoffrey hoped it was the former. When he had thought about their encounter he had envisaged it taking place in some motorway cafeteria where Roger had stopped for breakfast. Daylight broke over Surbiton. He must have made himself something to eat. But even so he would stop for a cup of coffee, surely, at some stage in his journey?

It was just after seven when the front door opened. Geoffrey saw Michaels's back as he closed the door, then a side view as he walked to the garage. Middle height, little moustache, firm walk. Geoffrey fingered his car keys as he heard the garage doors opened. Then another wait. What was the man *doing*? Finally a car started and began backing out.

The rush of blood to Geoffrey's head was so blinding he had to lean against a tree. It was a silver-blue Honda. There it stood, in the middle of the road, as Roger got out to close the garage doors. A silver-blue Honda. He had killed her. Deliberately run her down. The coincidence was too glaring to believe otherwise. Suddenly decisive, Geoffrey ran to his car, started it, and when the Honda had driven past, silently put it into gear and followed at a safe distance.

All the way, through suburb after dreary suburb and towards the M1, Geoffrey was thinking. He had tried to throw her over, and she had not taken it lying down. She had got troublesome. She had threatened to go to his wife. He could not imagine Helen being troublesome, but then the whole of Helen's other life was something he could only conceive of by imagining a quite different sort of woman. She was a woman of forty, hopelessly in love with a younger man. A desperate woman will adopt desperate means. He on the other hand had simply been having a fling on the side. His marriage was important to him. Why? Did the wife have money?

Helen had been driven down between town and home, on a stretch of highway where a spurt of speed was possible. She had been giving her cookery class as usual—something she always did on a Tuesday night. Anyone could have known this, but it was something Michaels would doubtless have known very well. He must have driven down from the North, parked there, waited for her to pass, then driven into her at speed and driven on. Geoffrey felt that great, choking well of anger in him, still as strong as when he had seen the car.

At last they got to the motorway. Roger was not a fast lane man, Geoffrey was relieved to find. He kept on the inside, driving carefully. Was he naturally a fast lane man, but one with something on his mind? On and on they went, towards the Midlands, towards the North. He was not going to stop! Geoffrey felt a growing surge of frustration, pushing his anger to boiling point. He was not going to stop! Where was he going to be able to confront him? Tell him face to face that he knew what he had done?

They were nearing a flyover. On an impulse he accelerated. He drew level with the Honda and stayed level. Roger was driving steadily, carefully. A flicker crossed his face. He had realized that the car beside him in the next lane had been there too long. He turned his head, and saw Geoffrey's face looking directly at him. Geoffrey saw his jaw drop. Michaels had recognized him. So Helen had shown him pictures. His jaw was working. He seemed about to say something. Then all of a sudden his car was out of control, swerving to the left, off the road, through the flyover's safety barrier and down to the ground or road beneath. Geoffrey's last view had been of a face crazed with terror.

He drove on till he came to a lay-by. He sat for some minutes with his head in his hands. He had done nothing. His car had not touched the Honda. And yet—what had been his motive in driving up beside him, staying beside him in the second lane? To get a good look? Or with the subconscious desire that something like this would happen?

At any rate, some kind of justice had been done. Ten minutes later, almost cool again, Geoffrey drove to the next junction, then turned and headed South. There were police and AA men on the flyover, and down below he could hear the shriek of an ambulance.

Geoffrey drove to Surbiton on the next Saturday, to buy a local paper. There was a brief notice of the accident, with the news that it had involved no other deaths, though a passenger was injured in a car on the road below which had been slightly grazed by the falling Honda. Geoffrey was relieved it was not worse. He went back to Surbiton the next Saturday, and the one after that, but it was not till the third Saturday that he found a report of the inquest.

The Coroner, before accepting a verdict of accidental death, set out the facts admirably. The dead man was still young, was happily married, and had quite recently embarked on a promising career with a first-rate company. Unfortunately his job necessitated a great deal of travelling. There was no evidence that Mr Michaels had been drinking, either on the morning, or the night before. Nor was there any evidence that his judgment could have been impaired for any other reason—for example drugs. The relevant facts were that Mr Michaels had not had a great deal of sleep the night before, and had begun his long journey early in the morning. It was clear that the accident had been caused by a momentary lapse in concentration.

The Coroner also noted the fact that in her evidence Roger Michaels's widow had suggested that a contributory factor in the accident was the fact that her husband was driving a car to which he was not accustomed. His company Volvo was in the garage for an extensive refit, and he had been forced to take her car.

A BUSINESS PARTNERSHIP

Everyone said they made a marvellous threesome, because somehow they balanced each other. The Chatterways were so smart and healthy and glamorous: they always looked tanned, obviously had some kind of home gym, and dressed with an unostentatious rightness. Put like that it might suggest they were priggish or inhuman, but in fact they were anything but that. They were enormous fun to be with, and so pleasant on the eye that an invitation from them—and they entertained a lot—was something to be cherished, looked forward to expectantly.

Paul, on the other hand, was shambling: untidy, even unkempt, with flecks of paint on his clothes and hands, and a layer of nicotine on his teeth. He sometimes drank too much, and certainly never went to a tailor's. Paul nicely dispelled any idea people might have had that the Chatterways were too perfect.

Of course technically there was no reason to consider them a threesome at all. Paul had the flat in David and Imogen's house—Meadowbanks, their large, modern house of Scandinavian inspiration, where the light in the flat lifted Paul's painter's heart. He had been at school with David, and now painted precise, painterly landscapes of a conservative kind which sold well, yet somehow belied his public personality. David was head of a furniture business that specialized in modern pieces, all quality wood and clean lines.

Yet it was not surprising that they were regarded as a threesome, or that people, when they invited the Chatterways to dinner, always added: 'You'll bring Paul along too, won't you?' For Paul usually did come (necessitating unexpected invitations to divorcées or widows who thought they had in their solitude been entirely dropped by their former friends), and he was always to be seen in their company: if they went shopping in Leamington Spa he would go with them, and they'd meet up for lunch. At concerts and fêtes they would usually arrive together, and they were often to be seen on drives around the countryside on Sundays, when David and Imogen might sit reading, while Paul made sketches. If you were invited to the Chatterways you would expect Paul to be there, but if you dropped in unexpectedly during the evening you would probably find him there then too—sprawled in the long, uncluttered sitting-room, smoking his old pipe. You could say that Paul earthed the Chatterways.

Naturally people, being human, made the odd joke, the occasional conjecture. They said that Paul had gone on their honeymoon with them; they suggested he was the emasculated male figure of fiction and of real life—the Turgenev to their Viardots, hopelessly in love with Imogen. Some said he was in love with David—weren't they at public school together, after all? Some, under their breath, suggested they all shared a bed together, in a variation of the pattern favoured by Sir Charles Dilke (the comparison sprang to mind because David and Imogen were active in Liberal circles).

No one hit on the truth: that at the end of the day spent running David's home, entertaining David's friends, establishing David's role in the community and significantly helping him to run his business, the bed Imogen went to was Paul's.

It was an ideal working arrangement. David needed a wife in the social sense—a helpmeet who was also an ornament. His sexual drives were low, intermittent, and essentially solitary. Paul needed a bed-partner, but he had no use for a wife who would be around him at all hours. He knew Imogen at once most intimately and least intimately. Imogen loved money, good clothes and good food, the sense

of living luxuriously, though hers was also a generous nature
—a spreader of good fortune rather than a hoarder of it.
She also liked spice and a mild sense of danger. The joke
people made about their honeymoon was not too far from
the truth. Paul had flown to Pisa by a different flight, and
they had all met up outside Customs. While David had
taken his hired car to Florence, Paul and Imogen had driven
in theirs to Portofino. They had all enjoyed themselves very
much.

In fact, they enjoyed their life together very much too.
A typical day might have Imogen entertaining important
foreign buyers to lunch. She was a delightful hostess—
impeccable in her standards, yet relaxed and amusing. She
was a beautiful woman, and if a hair on her head was never
out of place, nor did her coiffure seem to have been bulldozed
into conformity. David, with his lithe, broad-shouldered
figure, his even but not ostentatious tan, seemed almost
un-English to his guests (who were much more used to
British businessmen of the pot-bellied and guzzling variety).
The Chatterways were like their furniture: the quality of
the product was undeniable.

Often they entertained David's employees. These were
big do's, and outside caterers were called in. But always
there were special dishes that Imogen had cooked or prepared, and the flower arrangements were hers alone. And
the welcome she gave—she and David gave—made everyone from board director to workshop sweeper feel at home,
wanted, part of one big team.

And when the workers from Chatterway and Company
had gone home, Imogen would go to Paul's bed—cool,
delightful, responsive.

It was a surprise to Imogen when she became pregnant.
She was, after all, thirty-nine—she had been over thirty
when she had married David. They had never intended
having children, and she or Paul had always taken pre-
cautions.

Well, almost always.

'I can see it's not something you've been working or hoping for,' said Dr McLintock.

Working for—what an odd phrase, thought Imogen.

'Well, not exactly.'

'If you should decide you don't want it, there's your age—'

'Yes. Can I have a few days to think it over?'

'Oh, of course. Though the sooner you make the decision the better, naturally. At your age . . .'

Really, thought Imogen, driving home, he did rather go on about my age. Because there's no reason at all why I *shouldn't* have it, now it's in there, waiting. It's not as though Paul were black or anything, so that the game would be up. No reason why there should be any talk at all. Everyone would be delighted for us. The question is whether I want all the pain, the bother, the responsibility. That's all.

Though in fact it wasn't quite all.

She decided not to tell 'her boys' (was it significant she thought of them like that?) until she had made her decision. Paul and David were both conscious that something was 'up', because of Imogen's quietness, her secretive smile. They thought she was preparing some surprise, or joke— one of those little things she occasionally did that added piquancy to their lives together.

She announced it to them a couple of evenings later at dinner, over escargots.

'You're not going to believe this, you two—' (again, was it significant that her phrasing made it sound like a speech from a school story?)—'but I'm pregnant.'

There was a brief silence, then David laughed.

'You're *not*. But you're always boasting how careful—'

'A momentary lapse,' said Imogen.

'Beastly of me to laugh,' said David, relaxing. 'I believe abortions are nasty, messy things.'

Imogen began clearing away the plates.

'I'm not having an abortion.'

She caught the look of horror on both their faces before she went to the kitchen.

'You're not serious,' Paul said, when she came back with the casserole.

'Yes, I am. I've decided to have it.'

Her coolness irritated them enormously, as did her assumption that it was her decision alone.

'But you've never wanted a child,' protested David. 'It was part of the agreement.'

'No, I've never felt in the least maternal before, I agree. Now, on balance, I want to keep it.'

'Well, I've never felt in the least dynastic,' said David forcefully. 'When I'm bored with the business, I want to sell it at a gigantic profit and retire. Children never do what their parents want them to do these days anyway. You go through the nappy stage, and the first bike stage, then pimples and young love, and when you're just about to hand over the family firm to them, they tell you they want to go and administer famine relief in Africa. No thank you.'

'Have you thought of all the bother?' asked Paul. 'All the wailing and screaming, the need to feed it, the disturbed nights, the nappy-changing? Have you realized what that's going to do to your life?'

'You mean what it's going to do to your life,' said Imogen. 'Can anyone eat any more of this casserole?'

That was typical of Imogen's behaviour over the next few days. As soon as David or Paul attempted to discuss the subject with her, remind her of their agreement, point out the changes a baby would bring to their lifestyle, she coolly changed the subject. She seemed to imply—and both men thought it rather outrageous of her—that it was a question for herself alone to decide, and that she had decided it.

'The whole arrangement was working like a dream,' said David to Paul, over a lunch-time pint at a country pub near the factory headquarters. 'And now she's brought the thing down round our ears with a vengeance! Diarrhœa and nappy-rash—'

'Burps and colic—'

'Shopping at Mothercare and agitating for more nursery-schools—'

'And the little bugger screaming its heart out most of the day, chucking its pap on the carpet and banging its spoon on the high chair. My God!'

'It used to be such a peaceful house,' said David. 'Orderly, in the classical sense.'

'I need peace and order,' said Paul. 'For my work.'

But there didn't seem a lot they could do about it. Imogen simply didn't discuss the matter with them, beyond a few pieces of news about the progress of the pregnancy. 'Dr McLintock was quite pleased with me today,' or, 'I can't wait to feel the little monster kick—' that was about the extent of it. As time passed the question of an abortion simply faded away. The men felt bruised, discarded, as if they had been used, and then cast aside.

'If we divorced,' said David, 'it'd be me she'd sue for maintenance of the child. She knows which side her bread is buttered on.'

Meanwhile, though she cut down a little on her work around the house—made simpler meals, bought convenience foods—she still entertained with zest, and enjoyed her work in the community. What Paul and David suspected she enjoyed most about these activities were people's delighted comments on her pregnancy, and the possibility of comparing notes about its progress with women who had already had children.

'I'm terrified of losing it,' she confided to one of these women.

'Oh, darling, not in this day and age.'

But both of them knew the possibility still existed in this day and age.

Imogen paid frequent visits (she and David were private

patients, of course) to Dr McLintock, and during them she confided not only all her symptoms, but all her fears. Sometimes she caught a shadow crossing his face that suggested that his fears echoed her fears. He said nothing, but Imogen was an intelligent woman, and McLintock knew he couldn't get away with pooh-poohing the natural fears of a woman who was having a first baby at thirty-nine.

'I don't like pumping drugs into people,' he said, 'particularly pregnant women. But Mylexadrin I was going to prescribe anyway—I always do with an over-thirty who is having a first child. It has an excellent record in making sure the pregnancy runs its full course.'

Imogen was helping at a Liberal Bring and Buy Sale the next day. A General Election was in the offing, and as always Liberals were hopeful of a great triumph for middle-of-the-roadery. Their home village, near Leamington Spa, was an old-fashioned part of the country, full of retired professional people, and David made the joke that they called the Bingo in Latin numerals. But Liberals were oddly abundant, and Imogen enjoyed herself. She had a stall where she could sit down all afternoon, and plenty of volunteers to relieve her. On the way in with David and Paul she gave her husband Dr McLintock's prescription.

'Be a dear and pick this up for me.'

'Of course. What is it?'

'Oh—pregnancy pills,' said Imogen, shrugging.

Paul's eyes met David's briefly in the driving mirror.

'Something for the little woman's interesting condition,' said David facetiously as he handed over the prescription at the chemist's.

'Oh yes, Mylexadrin,' said the dispenser. 'We stock it. Very useful little drug for the older woman—though I shouldn't call your good lady that, should I?'

'What does it do?' asked David casually, his eyes exploring the range of cough lozenges on the counter in front of him.

'Works against premature birth or miscarriage. Always

a danger in these circumstances. Don't want any accidents at this stage, do we?'

'We certainly don't,' said David.

Paul followed him out of the shop. In the car they examined the tablets.

'They look just like the indigestion tablets Dr McLintock prescribed for me last year,' said David. 'Very mild, quite harmless.'

Without further discussion they headed for home. When David handed over the bottle to Imogen at the end of the Sale, he said:

'It's got one of those damned anti-child tops. You never can work them. There. That's it.'

But Imogen would probably never have noticed that the bottle had been opened. She was quite unsuspicious, living in her own little world.

The crisis came in the seventh month. By then the men had almost despaired of its ever coming, though they had not resigned themselves to the baby. David was weighing up the pros and cons of suing for adultery on the grounds of Imogen's affair with Paul. Paul had decided he thoroughly disliked sleeping with a pregnant woman, and was considering moving out—wonderful light for a painter at Meadowbanks or no. Then, on a filthy night in October, over the sound of pelting rain, David heard a scream.

It was a *Jane Eyre* touch quite unsuited to the cool Finnish expansiveness of Meadowbanks. He turned on the bedside light and leapt out of bed. He heard scrambled footsteps down the stairs from the split-level flat that Paul inhabited, then the connecting door opening.

'David! David!'

It's come, thought David. Together they ran up to Paul's bedroom. Imogen was on the bed, hunched over, alternately screaming and moaning, the screams so terrible it seemed they must cut through the teeming rain and be heard in the village.

'Get a doctor! . . . Christ! Oh, my God! . . . No, call 999. Get an ambulance . . . AHHH!'

'That's it,' said David. 'We'll call an ambulance right away. It's a hospital matter. We'll just get you downstairs first.'

'No! Call the frigging ambulance!'

'Don't be silly, Imogen,' said David reasonably. 'You can't be found in Paul's bed. Come along.'

'I don't care whose bloody bed I'm found in,' screamed Imogen, hardly recognizable as the cool, witty hostess of Meadowbanks. Her face was red with pain and effort, her hair torn, her whole body wrenched out of shape. 'Call that ambulance!'

'Come along,' they both said. 'Only a few steps. It's not far. We'll soon have the ambulance men out when we've got you into David's bed. They'll know what to do. They're used to this kind of thing.'

Dumbly, bent with pain, Imogen stood up, recognizing that she had no choice. Immediately she lunged forward. Her body felt as if a burning iron had been thrust into it. David's strength saved her. He took one arm, very gently, and Paul the other, and slowly, slowly, they got her through the studio, down the stairs—each one a screaming, torturing effort for Imogen—and then across the wide, pine-lined landing to David's bedroom. When they had settled her for the first time in David's bed, David said: 'Now I'll ring 999.'

Was it Imogen's tortured imagination, measuring minutes by hideous, lunging pain, or was it a long, long time before David returned and said they were on their way?

The ambulance men were very efficient, but there was little they could do to ease Imogen's agony. The rain didn't help, enforcing redoubled care on the driver. The crisis came in the ambulance, and David and Paul were very glad they had decided to follow in David's Volvo. By the time the stretcher was carried into the Maternity Wing, it held only a dead child, cradled beside a dead mother.

David and Paul genuinely grieved. 'I can't express our sense of loss and grief,' David wrote to a friend, and neither David nor the friend found it odd that he should write in the plural. Paul and he sat together in the evenings, watching television or listening to music, and they ate together the meals left to be warmed up in the oven by the woman who came in from the village. Often they said: 'If *only* she hadn't got that scatterbrained idea . . .'

David entertained buyers and contacts at various restaurants in Leamington, and as often as not Paul came along too. When David had his employees over to Meadowbanks for the annual get-together the usual caterers were employed, but this time they did everything. The employees shook their heads in private, and said it was wonderful of David to make the effort, but somehow it wasn't quite the same.

The occasion was memorable to David and Paul, however. Both of them, quite independently, noticed a new girl who had recently joined the marketing division. She was fair, pretty, and stood around on that hot summer's day as if the sun had no power over her. She looked, David said, as if she belonged.

Her name was Evelyn, and she was surprised when she was invited to dinner. David told her to tell nobody, so she hugged to herself the notion that promotion was in the offing. It was in fact at the end of the meal, during which David had noted again how perfectly Evelyn had behaved, that over fresh strawberries the matter was broached.

'We'd like to make a proposition to you,' David said, 'entirely in confidence. It's a little unusual, and if you don't accept, you must just forget about it entirely. You see, we've noticed, both of us, how well you seem to fit in here . . .'

Evelyn listened, at first astounded, then fascinated, then

seeing the beautiful logic and suitability of the arrangement. It was a wonderful house—a dream house for someone who loved open space and clean lines. And David—well, everyone at work had been in love with David, and Evelyn was no exception: that lean, athletic, fined-down look, which went with his beautiful courtesy and consideration. Odd that he shouldn't be more . . . interested. But Paul, if he was not good-looking, was still a roly-poly bundle of a man, awfully pleasant and comfortable. Paul would do to have David's baby by.

Because she didn't take seriously all that stuff about not wanting children. Of course when it came down to it David would want an heir for the business. Men always did. He'd just been thrown off-balance by that awful business with his wife. A clever girl could always devise ways of finding herself pregnant, couldn't she? For Evelyn did want a child more than anything in the world.

LITTLE TERROR

It was Albert Wimpole's first holiday on his own for—oh, he didn't know how long: since he was in his late 'teens it must have been. Because after Mum died, Dad always liked to tag along with him, and though Dad was quite lively, and certainly no trouble at all, still, it was not quite the same, because Albert was a considerate person, conscientious, and naturally he adapted a lot to Dad's ways. Now Dad had decided, regretfully, that he couldn't quite manage it this year, his arthritis being what it was. So Albert was going to enjoy Portugal on his own. A small thrill of anticipation coursed through his slightly old-maidish veins. Who knew what adventures he might meet with? What encounters he might have? On the first day, though, he decided not to go down to the Carcavelos beach, because the breeze was rather high. At the hotel pool it was nice and sheltered.

'Hello.'

The voice came from behind his ear. Albert's heart sank, but he was a courteous man, and he turned round on his sun-bed in order to respond. He saw, without joy, a pink, ginger-haired boy, with evilly curious eyes.

'Hello,' said Albert, and began to turn back.

'How old are you?'

'How old? Let me see now . . . I'm forty-two.'

The carroty boy thought.

'That's not three score years and ten, is it?'

'No, it's not, I'm glad to say. In fact, it's not much more than half way there.'

'*I've* not even used up the ten,' said the child.

'I can see that. You've got an awful lot left.'

'Yes. Still, I wouldn't say you were *old*, yet,' said the boy.

'Thank you very much,' said Albert, and turned over

thankfully as the boy left, but not before he had caught sight of the boy's parents, waving in his direction in a friendly fashion. They were heavy, unattractive people of about his own age, or older. Perhaps the Menace was a late blessing, the result of some virulent fertility drug, and spoilt accordingly.

When Albert had been by the pool a couple of hours, he got ready to leave. No sense in overdoing the sunshine on the first day of your holiday. You pay for that if you do, Dad always said, and he was right. As he was just preparing to make his move, the ginger-haired head appeared once more close to his.

'What's your name?'

'My name's Wimpole. What's yours?'

'Terry.'

'Ah—short for "Terror", I suppose.'

'No, it isn't, silly. It's short for Terence. Everybody knows that. And I think Wimpole is a jolly funny name. Do you know what happens to you when you die?'

The abrupt change in the topic caught Albert on the hop, and he paused a moment before replying.

'That's something people have been discussing for quite a long time.'

'No, it's not, stupid. You lie there still, and you don't breathe, and you don't even twitch, and you don't have dreams, because you're dead.'

'I see. Yes, I did know that.'

'Then they put you in a box, and either they put you in the ground and throw earth all over you, or they cre-mate you. That means they burn you up, like Guy Fawkes night.'

'I must be getting along,' said Albert, and indeed he did begin to feel a burning sensation on his shoulders.

'You know, you don't necessarily die at three score years and ten.'

'That's a comfort.'

'My Gran was seventy-four, and that's more, isn't it? My friend Wayne Catherick said she was past it.'

'Well, it's nice to think I might stagger on a bit longer than seventy,' said Albert, who had gathered together his things and now began to make his way out.

'Terry's taken quite a fancy to you,' said Little Terror's parents as he walked past them. Albert smiled politely.

The next morning Albert ventured on the beach. He walked half a mile towards the fortress, then laid out his towel and settled down. At first the breeze worried him a little, because he knew people often sunburned badly in a breeze, but by half past ten it had died down, and things had become quite idyllic.

'There's Wimpole!' came the well-known voice. Against his wiser instincts Albert looked up. Terry was standing over him, and pointing, as if he were some unusual sea creature.

'We won't intrude,' said Terry's parents, settling themselves down two or three yards away, and beginning to remove clothes from their remarkably ill-proportioned bodies. Terry, however, intruded.

While his parents just lay there tanning those fleshy bodies of theirs (Albert prided himself on keeping in good trim), Terry confined himself to questions like 'What's that?' and to giving information about his friend Wayne Catherick. When his parents went down to dabble their toes in the freezing Atlantic, Terry's conversation reverted to the topics of yesterday.

'When you're cre-mated,' he said, 'they shoot your body into a great big oven. Then when you're all burnt up, they put the ashes into a bottle, and you can put flowers in front of it if you want to.'

'I think I'll be buried.'

'Or they can scatter the ashes somewhere. Like over Southend, or into the sea, or over Scotland. Do you know what Wayne says, Wimpole?'

'No. What does Wayne say?'

'He says my gran's ashes ought to have been scattered over Tesco's supermarket, because she ate so much.'

'That's a very nasty thing for Wayne to say.'

'No, it's not. It's true, Wimpole. She was eating us out of house and home. Wayne says she took the food from out of our mouths. She just sat up there in her bedroom, eating. Sometimes I had to go up and get her tray, and she hadn't finished, and it was disgusting. She used to spray me with bits. I could have had chocolate cream sponge every day if she hadn't taken the food from out of my mouth.'

'I don't think chocolate cream sponge every day would have been very good for you.'

'Yes, it would. *And* I had to keep quiet, *every* morning and *every* night because she was a*sleep*. It wasn't fair.'

'You *have* made a hit,' said Terry's mother, coming back. 'It's nice for you, seeing as you're on your own, isn't it?'

The next day Albert waited in his room until he saw them trailing down to the beach. Then he made his way to the pool, and gratefully sank down on a lilo. Though his sunbathing had been in shorter doses than he had intended, the red was beginning to turn to a respectable brown. Half an hour later Terry was sitting beside him, telling him about Wayne.

'It was awfully breezy on the beach,' Terry's dad called out, in a friendly way. 'You were wise to come here.'

'Wayne's dad has a sports shop,' said Terry. 'I got my costume there. Wayne's got an Auntie Margaret and two grannies. His grannies aren't dead!' he ended emphatically, as if he had scored a definite point there.

'That's nice,' said Albert. 'Grannies are always nice to little boys, aren't they?'

'Ha!' said Little Terror, latching back on to his grievance with the tenacity of a politician. 'Mine wasn't, Wimpole. I had to be as quiet as quiet, all the time. And her up there stuffing food into her mouth and dribbling, and spitting out crumbs. I don't call that nice. It was disgusting. I was glad when she died and they put her in the oven.'

'I'm sure that your Mummy and Daddy would be very upset if they heard you say that.'

'That's why I don't say it when they're there,' said Terry, simply. 'I expect they quite wanted her to live.'

The next day Albert went to the beach at Estoril, then caught the bus to Sintra in the afternoon. When he got back to the hotel the dinner-hour was almost over, and Terry and his parents were tucking into enormous slices of caramel cake.

'We missed you today,' said Terry's mum, reproachfully, as he passed their table.

When Terry's parents got up to go, they came over and introduced themselves properly. They were the Mumfords, they said. And they had something to ask Albert.

'One doesn't like *putting* on people, but Terry's so fond of you, and it is a *bit* difficult shopping with him tagging along, and we wondered if you *could* keep an eye on him one afternoon so we could go into Lisbon. After all, it's not much fun for a child, watching his parents trying on shoes, is it?'

Albert thought the request an outrageous one. All his instincts cried out against agreeing. Why should he ruin a day of his holidays looking after someone else's repellent (and tedious) child? All his natural instincts told him to say no. All his middle-class instincts told him he had to say yes. He said yes.

'Let me see—I have places I'm planning to go to, and some friends I have to see—' he improvised, untruthfully.

'Oh—friends in Portugal,' said Mrs Mumford, in a tone of voice which seemed to be expressing either scepticism or disapproval.

'Shall we say Monday?'

Monday was five days away, and the Mumfords would obviously have preferred some earlier day, but *their* middle-class instincts forced them not to quibble, but to accept and to thank him gratefully.

The next day was a day of rest for Albert: the Mumfords went on one of the tours—to Nazaré and Fatima. When he

went past their table at dinner-time, Mrs Mumford en-
thused to him about the shrine of Fatima.

'It was a real religious experience,' she said. 'I expect
Terry will want to tell you about it.'

Albert repressed a shudder, out of consideration for any
Portuguese waiter who might be listening. He merely smiled
and went on to his table.

The next day he took the train to Queluz, and the day
after he spent exploring the little back streets of Lisbon,
then in the afternoon walking up the broad avenue to the
park. But all the time Monday was approaching inexorably,
and short of going down with beri-beri, Albert could see
no way of avoiding his stewardship of the repulsive and
necrophilic Terry.

On Monday morning (it turned out, without explanation,
to be a whole day's shopping Terry's parents were planning), after the Mumfords had trailed off towards the train
for Lisbon, Albert took Terry into Carcavelos and filled him
unimaginably full of ice-cream. He hoped it would make
him ill or sleepy, but it did neither. When Albert suggested
a very light lunch, Terry demanded roast pork at one of the
town's little restaurants. Portions were substantial, and he
ate with gusto. All this eating at least kept him quiet. Far
from responding to suggestions that he have an afternoon's
nap, Terry demanded to be taken to the hotel swimming
pool. Terry's parents had impressed upon Albert most
forcefully that Terry was not allowed to use the diving-
board, but while Albert was still fussing around removing
his own clothes, he saw that Terry was already up there,
and preparing to throw himself into the water.

'This is a suicide dive!' yelled the child. 'I want to be
cremated!'

'You've got to be drowned first,' muttered Albert. Ten
seconds later he was in the pool, fishing out the sobbing,
gasping boy. Respect for the susceptibilities of parents prevented Albert giving him a good smacking, but he was able

to pummel him pretty satisfyingly on the pretext of getting
water out of his lungs. He commanded him to lie still for at
least ten minutes.

'Would I be in heaven now, if I had drowned, Wimpole?'
Terry asked, after five.

Albert did not think it wise to go into alternative desti-
nations for his soul. His parents might be namby-pamby as
theologians.

'I believe there is some period of waiting.'

'Like on the platform, before the train comes in?' asked
Terry. 'I bet once I started I'd have gone fast. Like a
space-shot. Whoosh! You wouldn't have been able to see
me, I'd have gone so fast.'

'I expect you're right,' said Albert, reading his P.D. James.

'I bet Grandma didn't go fast like that. I can't see it. She
was enormous. Wayne's mum called her un-wiel—'

'Unwieldy.'

'That's right. It means enormous. Colossal. Like a great,
fat pig.'

'You know your mother wouldn't like hearing you say
that.'

'She isn't here,' said Terry dismissively. 'Anyway, you
can't expect to go to heaven like a space-shot if you eat
enough for three elephants. *And* if you're bad-tempered and
make everyone's life a misery.'

Terry lay quiet for a bit, watching other children in the
pool, children with whom he habitually refused to play.
Then, out of the corner of his eye, Albert was aware that he
was being watched, slyly, out of the corner of Terry's eye.

'My grandma died of an overdose,' Terry said.

'An overdose of you?' asked Albert, though he knew it
was useless to venture humour on this horrible child.

'No, stupid. An overdose of medicine. She had it in a
glass by the side of her bed, so she could take it while
Mummy was out at work. Mummy does half days at the
librerry. And Gran's medicine was left in the glass by her

bed. So she didn't have to get up and go to any trouble to get it. Fat old pig!'

'Terry—if I hear any more words like that about your gran I'm going to take you and lock you in your room. In fact, I don't wish to hear any more about your gran at all.'

'All right,' said Terry equably. 'Only it's funny the medicine was in the cupboard, and she'd have to get up and get it to give herself an overdose, isn't it? 'Cos it was left by her bed like that every day.'

'I expect she felt bad, and thought she needed more,' suggested Albert.

'Maybe,' said Terry.

Then he took himself off once more to the pool, and began showing off in front of the smaller children. Before very long he was on the diving-board again, and Albert was in the pool rescuing him. It was during the third time this happened that the Mumfords arrived back at the hotel.

'I do hope he hasn't been any trouble,' said Mrs Mumford. 'Now say thank you to Mr Wimpole, Terry.'

For the remainder of the holiday the sun shone with a terrible brightness. Albert grew inventive about where he spent his days. He took the bus and ferry out to Sesimbra, he found little beaches on the Estoril coast where fishermen still mended their nets and tourists were never seen. He took the train up to Coimbra, and only rejected Oporto because he calculated that he would only have two hours to spend there before he would have to travel back. He had none of the spicy or sad romantic adventures he had hoped for—what lonely, middle-aged person does on holiday, unless he pays for them?—but he arrived back at the hotel for dinner tired and not dissatisfied with his days.

'My, you *have* got a lot of friends in Portugal,' said the Mumfords who were now spending all their days by the pool. 'We've made good friends with Manuel, the waiter there,' explained Dad Mumford. 'He's introduced us to this lovely restaurant run by his uncle. They're wonderful to

Terry there, and they really do us proud at lunch-time.'

So the Mumfords had found they could do without him.

Eventually it was time to go home. On the bus to the airport Albert hung back, and selected a seat well away from Terry. At the airport there was a slight delay, while the plane was refuelled and cleaned, and restocked with plastic food. In any case, Albert knew that there he would not be able to escape the Mumfords entirely.

'Do you think you could just keep an eye on Terry for one *min*ute while we go to the Duty Free Shop?' his mum asked. There was something in the tone of voice as she asked it, as if she knew he had considered their earlier request an encroachment, and she regretted having to ask again so obviously selfish a person.

'Of course,' said Albert.

'I'll tell you how she died,' said Terry, as their heavy footsteps faded away across the marble halls.

'I don't wish to know.'

'Yes, you do. She was lying up there, and Wayne and I were playing in my bedroom—*quiet*ly. How can you play quietly? And we were pretty fed up. And she called out, and called, and called. And when we went in, she said she'd got stuck on one side, and couldn't get over, and her leg had gone to sleep. She hadn't had her afternoon medicine yet. And while Wayne pretended to push her, I got the bottle from the cupboard, and I emptied some of it into her glass, and then I put it back in the cupboard. Then I went and pushed with Wayne, and finally we got her over. She said she was ever so grateful. She said, "Now I can go off." We laughed and laughed when we got back to my room. She went off all right!'

'I'm not believing any of this, Terry.'

'Believe it or not, I don't care,' said Terry. 'It's true. That's how the old pig died.'

'It's an awful swindle in there,' said the Mumfords, coming back from the Duty Free Shop. 'Hardly any cheaper than in England. I shouldn't bother to go.'

'I'll just take a look,' said Albert, escaping.

Albert did not enjoy his flight home at all, though he bought no less than three of the little bottles of white wine they sell with the meal. He was examining the story and re-examining it with the brain of one who was accustomed to weighing up stories likely and unlikely (for Albert worked in a tax office). On the face of it, it was incredible—that a small boy (or was it two small boys?) should kill someone in this simple, almost foolproof way. Yet there had been in the last few years murder cases—now and again, yet often enough—involving children horribly young. And in England too, not in America, where people like Albert imagined such things might be common occurrences.

Albert shook his head over the stewed fish that turned out to be braised chicken. How was he to tell? And if he said nothing, how terrible might be the consequences that might ensue! If adult murderers are inclined to kill a second time, how much more likely must a child be—one who has got away with it, and rejoices in his cleverness. Even the boy's own parents would not be safe, in the unlikely event of their ever crossing his will. What sort of figure would Albert make if he went to the police *then* with his story. Reluctantly, for he foresaw little but embarrassment and ridicule, Albert decided he would have to go to them and tell his tale. In his own mind he could not tell whether Little Terror's story was true or not. It would have to be left to trained minds to come to a conclusion.

At Gatwick Albert was first out of the plane, through Passport Control and Customs in no time, and out to his car, which was miraculously unscathed by the attentions of vandals or thieves. As he drove off towards Hull and home, Albert suddenly realized, with a little *moue* of distaste, that his holiday had had its little spice of adventure after all.

'Well!' said Terry's dad, when the police had finally left. 'We know who we have to thank for *that*!'

'There wasn't much point in keeping it secret, was there? He was the only one Terry talked to at all. And he seemed such a nice man!'

'I'm going to write him a stiff letter,' fumed Terry's dad. 'I know he works in the tax office in Hull. Interfering, trouble-making little twerp!'

'It could have been serious, you know. I hope you make him realize that. It could have been very embarrassing. If we hadn't been able to give him the names and addresses of *both* Terry's grannies . . . Oh, good Lord! What *are* they going to say?'

'The police are going to be very tactful. The Inspector told me so at the door. I think they'll probably just make inquiries of neighbours. Or pretend to be council workers, and get them talking. Just so's they make sure they are who we say they are.'

'*My* mother will find out,' said Mrs Mumford, with conviction and foreboding. 'She's got a nose! . . . And how am I going to explain it to her? I'll never forgive that Wimpole!'

Later that night, as they were undressing for bed, Terry's mum, who had been thinking, said to Terry's dad:

'Walter: you don't think we ought to have told them about Wayne Catherick's gran, do you?'

'What about her?'

'Old Mrs Corfitt, who lived next door. Should we have told them that she died of an overdose?'

'No. 'Course not. What's it to do with Terry? They said the old lady got confused and gave herself an extra lot.'

'I suppose it would just have caused more trouble,' agreed Mrs Mumford. 'And as you say, it was nothing to do with Terry, was it?'

She turned out the light.

'Well,' she said, as she prepared for sleep, 'I hope next time we go on holiday Terry finds someone nicer than *that* to make friends with!'

BREAKFAST TELEVISION

The coming of Breakfast Television has been a great boon to the British.

Caroline Worsley thought so anyway, as she sat in bed eating toast and sipping tea, the flesh of her arm companionably warm against the flesh of Michael's arm. Soon they would make love again, perhaps while the consumer lady had her spot about dangerous toys, or during the review of the papers, or the resident doctor's phone-in on acne. They would do it when and how the fancy took them—or as Michael's fancy took him, for he was very imperative at times—and this implied no dislike or disrespect for the breakfast-time performer concerned. For Caroline liked them all, and could lie there quite happily watching any one of them: David the doctor, Jason the pop-chart commentator, Selma the fashion expert, Jemima the problems expert, Reg the sports round-up man, and Maria the link-up lady. And of course Ben, the link-up man.

Ben, her husband.

It had all worked out very nicely indeed. Ben was called for by the studio at four-thirty. Michael always waited for half an hour after that, in case Ben had forgotten something and made a sudden dash back to the flat for it. Michael was a serious, slightly gauche young man, who would hate to be caught out in a situation both compromising and ridiculous. Michael was that rare thing, a studious student —though very well-built too, Caroline told herself appreciatively. His interests were work, athletics, and sex. It was Caroline who had initiated him into the pleasures of regular sex. At five o'clock his alarm clock went off, though as he told Caroline, it was rarely necessary. His parents were away in Africa, dispensing aid, know-how and Oxfam beatitudes in some godforsaken part of Africa, so he was alone in their flat. He put his tracksuit on, so that in the unlikely event of his being seen in the corridor he could pretend to be going running. But he never had been. By five past he was in Caroline's flat, and in the bedroom she shared with Ben. They had almost an hour and a half of sleeping and love-making before breakfast television began.

Not that Michael watched it with the enthusiasm of Caroline. Sometimes he took a book along and read it while Caroline was drawing in her breath in horror at combustible toys, or tut-tutting at some defaulting businessman who had left his customers in the lurch. He would lie there immersed in *The Mechanics of the Money Supply* or *Some Problems of Exchange-Rate Theory*—something reasonably straight-forward, anyway, because he had to read against the voice from the set, and from time to time he was conscious of Ben looking directly at him. He never quite got used to that.

It didn't bother Caroline at all.

'Oh look, his tie's gone askew,' she would say, or: 'You know, Ben's much balder than he was twelve months ago —I've never noticed it in the flesh.' Michael seldom man-aged to assent to such propositions with any easy grace. He was much too conscious of balding, genial, avuncular Ben, grinning out from the television screen, as he tried to wring from some graceless pop-star three words strung together consecutively that actually made sense. 'I think he's getting fatter in the face,' said Caroline, licking marmalade off her fingers.

'I am not getting fatter in the face,' shouted Ben. 'Balder, yes, fatter in the face definitely not.' He added in a voice soaked in vitriol: 'Bitch!'

He was watching a video of yesterday's love-making on a set in his dressing-room, after the morning's television session had ended. His friend Frank, from the technical staff, had rigged up the camera in the cupboard of his study, next door to the bedroom. The small hole that was necessary in the wall had been expertly disguised. Luckily Caroline was a deplorable housewife. Eventually she might have discovered the sound apparatus under the double bed, but even then she would probably have assumed it was some junk of Ben's that he had shoved there out of harm's way. Anyway, long before then . . .

Long before then—what?

'Hypocritical swine!' yelled Ben, as he heard Caroline laughing with Michael that the Shadow Foreign Secretary had really wiped the floor with him in that interview. 'She told me when I got home yesterday how well I'd handled it.'

As the shadowy figures on the screen turned to each other again, their bare flesh glistening dully in the dim light, Ben hissed: 'Whore!'

The make-up girl concentrated on removing the traces of powder from his neck and shirt-collar, and studiously avoided comment.

'I suppose you think this is sick, don't you?' demanded Ben.

'It's none of my business,' the girl said, but added: 'If she is carrying on, it's not surprising, is it? Not with the hours we work.'

'Not surprising? I tell you, I was bloody surprised! Just think how you would feel if your husband, or bloke, was two-timing you while you were at the studio.'

'He is,' said the girl. But Ben hadn't heard. He frequently didn't hear other people when he was off camera. His comfortable, sympathetic-daddy image was something that seldom spilled over into his private life. Indeed, at his worst, he could slip up even on camera: he could be leant forwards, listening to his interviewees with appearance of the warmest interest, then reveal by his next question that he hadn't heard a word they were saying. But that happened

very infrequently, and only when he was extremely preoccu-
pied. Ben was very good at his job.

'Now they'll have tea,' he said. 'Everyone needs a tea-
break in their working morning.'

Tea . . .

Shortly after this there was a break in Caroline's delicious
early-morning routine: her son Malcolm came home for a
long weekend from school. Michael became no more than
the neighbour's son, at whom she smiled in the corridor.
She and Malcolm had breakfast round the kitchen table.
It was on Tuesday morning, when Malcolm was due to
depart later in the day, that Ben made one of his little
slips.

He was interviewing Cassy Le Beau from the long-
running pop group The Crunch, and as he leaned forward
to introduce a clip from the video of their latest musical
crime, he said:

'Now, this is going to interest Caroline and Michael,
watching at home—'

'Why did he say Michael?' asked Caroline aloud, before
she could stop herself.

'He meant Malcolm,' said their son. 'Anyway, it's bloody
insulting, him thinking I'd be interested in The Crunch.'

Because Malcolm was currently rehearsing Elgar's
Second with the London Youth Orchestra. Ben was about
two years out of date with his interests.

'Did you see that yesterday morning?' Caroline asked
Michael, the next day.

'What?'

'Ben's slip on *Wake Up, Britain* yesterday.'

'I don't watch breakfast telly when I'm not with you.'

'Well, he did one of those "little messages home" that he
does—you probably don't remember, but there was all this
publicity about the families when *Wake Up, Britain* started,

and Ben got into the habit of putting little messages to Malcolm and me into the programme. Ever so cosy and ever so bogus. Anyway, he did one yesterday, as Malcolm was home, only he said "Caroline and Michael". Not Malcolm, but Michael.'

Michael shrugged.

'Just a slip of the tongue.'

'But his own *son*, for Christ's sake! And for the slip to come out as *Michael*!'

'These things happen,' said Michael, putting his arm around her and pushing her head back on to the pillow. 'Was there a Michael on the show yesterday?'

'There was Michael Heseltine on, as usual.'

'There you are, you see.'

'But Heseltine's an ex-cabinet minister. He would *never* call him Michael.'

'But the name was in his head. These things happen. Remember, Ben's getting old.'

'True,' said Caroline, who was two years younger than her husband.

'Old!' shouted Ben, dabbing at his artificially-darkened eyebrows, one eye on the screen. 'You think I'm old? I'll show you I've still got some bolts left in my locker.'

He had dispensed with the services of the make-up girl. He had been the only regular on *Wake Up, Britain* to demand one anyway, and the studio was surprised but pleased when Ben decided she was no longer required. Now he could watch the previous evening's cavortings without the damper of her adolescent disapproval from behind his shoulder.

And now he could plan.

One of the factors that just had to be turned to his advantage was Caroline's deplorable housekeeping. All the table-tops of the kitchen were littered with bits of this and that—herbs, spices, sauces, old margarine tubs, bits of jam on dishes. The fridge was like the basement of the Victoria and Albert Museum, and the freezer was a record of their married life. And on the window-ledge in the kitchen were the things he used to do his little bit of gardening . . .

Ben and Caroline inhabited one of twenty modern service flats in a block. Most of the gardening was done by employees of the landlords, yet some little patches were allotted to tenants who expressed an interest. Ben had always kept up his patch, though (as was the way of such things) it was more productive of self-satisfaction than of fruit or veg. 'From our own garden', he would say, as he served his guests horrid little bowls of red currants.

Already on the window-ledge in the kitchen there was a little bottle of paraquat.

That afternoon he pottered around in his mouldy little patch. By the time he had finished and washed his hands under the kitchen tap the paraquat had found its way next to the box of tea-bags standing by the kettle. The top of the paraquat was loose, having been screwed only about half way round.

'Does you good to get out on your own patch of earth,' Ben observed to Caroline, as he went through to his study.

The next question that presented itself was: when? There were all sorts of possibilities—including that the police would immediately arrest him for murder, he was reconciled to that—but he thought that on the whole it would be best to do it on the morning when he was latest home. Paraquat could be a long time in taking effect, he knew, but there was always a chance that they would not decide to call medical help until it was too late. If he was to come home to a poisoned wife and lover in the flat, he wanted them to be well and truly dead. Wednesday was the day when all the breakfast TV team met in committee to hear what was planned for the next week: which ageing star would be plugging her memoirs, which singer plugging his forthcoming British tour. Wednesdays Ben often didn't get home till early afternoon. Wednesday it was.

Tentatively in his mental engagements book he pencilled in Wednesday, May 15.

Whether the paraquat would be in the teapot of the Teasmade, or in the tea-bag, or how it would be administered, was a minor matter that he could settle long before the crucial Tuesday night when the tea-things for the morning had to be got ready. The main thing was that everything was decided.

May 15—undoubtedly a turning-point in her life—began badly for Caroline. First of all Ben kissed her goodbye before he set off for the studio, something he had not done since the early days of his engagement on breakfast television. Michael had come in at five o'clock as usual, but his love-making was forced, lacking in tenderness. Caroline lay there for an hour in his arms afterwards, wondering if anything was worrying him. He didn't say anything for some time—not till the television was switched on. Probably he relied on the bromides and the plugs to distract Caroline's attention from what he was going to say.

He had taken up his textbook, and the kettle of the Teasmade was beginning to hum, when he said, in his gruff, teenage way:

'Won't be much more of this.'

Caroline was watching clips from a Frank Bruno fight, and not giving him her full attention. When it was over, she turned to him:

'Sorry—what did you say?'

'I said there won't be much more of this.'

A dagger went to her heart, which seemed to stop beating for minutes. When she could speak, the words came out terribly middle-class-matron.

'I don't quite understand. Much more of what?'

'This. You and me together in the mornings.'

'You don't mean your parents are coming home early?'

'No. I've . . . got a flat. Nearer college. So there's not so much travelling in the mornings and evenings.'

'You're just *moving out*?'

'Pretty much so. Can't live with my parents for ever.'

Caroline's voice grew louder and higher.

'You're not living with your parents. It's six months before they come home. You're moving out *on me*. Do you have the impression that I'm the sort of person you can just move in with when it suits you, and then flit away from when it doesn't suit you any longer?'

'Well . . . yes, actually. I'm a free agent.'

'You *bas*tard! You *bas*tard!'

She would have liked to take him by the shoulder and shake him till the teeth rattled in his head. Instead she sat there on the bed, coldly furious. It was 7.15. The kettle whistled and poured boiling water on to the tea-bags in the teapot.

'Have some tea or coffee,' said Ben on the screen to his politician guest, with a smile that came out as a death's head grin. 'It's about early morning tea-time.'

'It's someone else, isn't it?' finally said Caroline, her voice kept steady with difficulty. 'A new girlfriend.'

'All right, it's a new girlfriend,' agreed Michael.

'Someone younger.'

'Of course someone younger,' said Michael, taking up his book again, and sinking into monetarist theory.

Silently Caroline screamed: *Of course someone younger*. What the hell's that supposed to mean? They don't come any older than you? Of course I was just passing the time with a crone like you until someone my own age came along?

'You're moving in with a girl,' she said, the desolation throbbing in her voice.

'Yeah,' said Michael, from within his Hayek.

'Tea all right?' Ben asked his guest.

Caroline sat there, watching the flickering images on the

screen, while the tea in the pot turned from hot to warm. The future spread before her like a desert—a future as wife and mother. What kind of life was that, for God's sake? For some odd reason a future as *lover* had seemed, when she had thought about it at all, fulfilling, traditional and dignified. Now any picture she might have of the years to come was turned into a hideous, mocking, negative image, just as the body beside her in the bed had turned from a glamorous sex object into a boorish, ungrateful teenager.

They were having trouble in the *Wake Up, Britain* studio, where the two anchor people had got mixed up as to who was introducing what. Caroline focused on the screen: she always enjoyed it when Ben muffed something.

'Sorry,' said Ben, smiling his kindly-uncle smile. 'I thought it was Maria, but in fact it's me. Let's see . . . I know it's David, our resident medico, but actually I don't know what your subject is today, David.'

'Poison,' said David.

But the camera had not switched to him, and the instant he dropped the word into the ambient atmosphere Caroline (and one million other viewers) saw Ben's jaw drop, and an expression of panic flash like lightning through his eyes.

'I've had a lot of letters from parents of small children,' said David, in his calm, everything-will-be-all-right voice, 'about what to do if the kids get hold of poison. Old medicines, household detergents, gardening stuff—they can all be dangerous, and some can be deadly.' Caroline saw Ben, the camera still agonizingly on him, swallow hard and put his hand up to his throat. Then, mercifully, the producer changed the shot at last to the doctor, leaning forward and doing his thing. 'So here are a few basic rules about what to do in that sort of emergency . . .'

Caroline's was not a quick mind, but suddenly a succession of images came together: Ben's kiss that morning, his smile as he offered his guest early morning tea, a bottle of paraquat standing next to the box of tea-bags in the kitchen, Ben's dropping jaw at the sudden mention of poison.

'Michael,' she said.

'What?' he asked, hardly bothering to take his head out of his book.

She looked at the self-absorbed, casually cruel body, and her blood boiled.

'Oh, nothing,' she said. 'Let's have tea. It'll be practically cold by now.'

She poured two cups, and handed him his. He put aside his book, which he had hardly been reading, congratulating himself in his mind on having got out of this so lightly. He took the cup, and sat on the bed watching the screen, where the sports man was now introducing highlights of last night's athletics meeting from Oslo.

'Boy!' said Michael appreciatively, stirring his tea. 'That was a great run!'

He took a great gulp of the tea, then hurriedly put the cup down, turned to look at Caroline, and then choked.

Caroline had not taken up her tea, but sat there looking at the graceless youth. Round her lips there played a smile of triumphal revenge—a smile that the camera whirring away in the secrecy of the study cupboard perfectly caught for Ben, and for the criminal court that tried them, ironically, together.

WHAT'S IN A NAME?

'Jeremy Fortescue?' Janice's mother had said in a voice shrill with horror. 'You most certainly are *not* engaged to Jeremy Fortescue! The man's a fornicator, a child-molester and a drunkard!'

'Not *that* Jeremy Fortescue,' said Janice.

It certainly was not. The well-known Jeremy Fortescue had become a British and international film star in the late 'sixties—an exciting image to suit the dangerous tastes of the time: square of shoulder, shirt open to the navel, a mocking smile on his lips that seemed both to invite women and to despise them for their inevitable fall. Byron's was the name most often invoked to describe both his persona and his private life which, as chronicled in the tabloids, suggested ruthlessness combined with an insatiable appetite for outré experience.

Janice's Jeremy Fortescue, the little-known one, was something in insurance and not anything very interesting in insurance at that. He was, on the other hand, a pudgy but likeable young man, and Janice's mother was soon quite happy about the engagement, though Janice's Jeremy always believed that she looked at him hard whenever he took a second drink, and imagined the other vices following in the train of drunkenness.

Even after five or six years of marriage Janice found that she had nothing much to complain of in the drink, fornication or child-molesting lines: the odd fumble at the office party, a *possible* dirty weekend away that she would like to be more sure about before she brought it up during a disagreement—these were very mild bumps on the high-way of a marriage. Really they were very happy. Children could wait until they were both more settled. Because Janice had a job with a local doctor, was active in the Conservative Association, and a keen tennis player. Added to which she was, as she put it, 'very much involved in things'.

Janice's mother had all her life been a great letter-writer, and the trait had descended to Janice. These were letters to council offices, firms, official bodies, national politicians: letters of complaint, protest, warning and admonishment. They were public-spirited letters, concerned letters. The tone of Janice's was more reasonable than her mother's: you could do an awful lot, she always said, if you kept the correspondence pleasant. She was not a busybody; she merely thought that people should do their job, and provide the services that they promised.

She found something out quite early in her career of public usefulness: she got much better results if she signed those letters Mrs Jeremy Fortescue. Mere Janice Fortescue would be treated politely enough by the bodies to which she had complained, but Mrs Jeremy Fortescue got results. Heaven knows what the feminist movement would say, she often said with a wry smile; but if it got street-lamps fixed, or proper policing in dangerous areas, well, wasn't it worth it? Janice loved to be able to point to results.

She also, as it happened, liked to get good service. And, after all, there was nothing *wrong* in using that form in personal matters as well, was there? When all was said and done, it *was* her name—that usage was perfectly all right, and had been very frequent twenty or thirty years ago. If a complaint to a shop or a ring to a plumber brought better service when you said 'Mrs Jeremy Fortescue', then why not say it? Janice knew her own mind, easily sorted out her moral priorities. She often chaired meetings of the Bridgehead Conservative Association and—young as she was—a lot of members thought of her as a bit of a tartar.

It was as Deputy Chairman of the Association that she went to Matching, one spring in the late 'seventies. The occasion was the spring meeting of the Conservative Associations of the South-West—not a terribly important meeting, but since the Chairman had another engagement Janice thought she'd like to go. Politics was about meeting people, wasn't it, so it seemed silly not to seize the opportunity. Matching was a lovely old town, and she looked it up in the AA book and telephoned for a room in the best hotel. This wasn't graft: she was paying for it herself. One did in the Bridgehead Conservative Association.

When she arrived in Matching she felt pleased with herself for her decision, and walked from the station through the lovely old town on a wave of euphoria. When she caught a sight of the Prince Frederick, a little off from the town centre, on a little square that had once been the market, she was pleased with her choice of hotel: it was a cool, spacious, eighteenth-century establishment that seemed to exhale the atmosphere of a more leisurely era. She put down her little suitcase, just to take in the elegant expanse of its frontage. Then she took it up again and marched confidently up to Reception.

'I have a room booked for the night.'

'Yes, madam: what name?'

'Mrs Jeremy Fortescue.'

'Oh, yes, of course, madam. It's 509. I have another key, just in case. Here we are. I do hope you'll find everything to your satisfaction, madam.'

Janice was hardly listening. She took the key, marched to the lift, and pressed the button for the fifth floor. How nice to be away for a time, and on one's own. Springy of step, she marched down the corridor and opened the door of 509.

'Hel-lo. What can I do for you?'

Janice had met her destiny, had had the encounter which her years of petty deceptions had been leading up to. Room 509 was in fact a most splendid suite, and he was standing by the door to the bathroom, glass in hand, close brown curly hair grown long over the collar, and dazzling white shirt open to the navel in a style that by now must have been second nature to him, so that to do up a few buttons would have seemed like being overdressed.

'Or could it be what would you care to do for me?' he added, with a dangerous yet somehow nervous smile.

'Oh dear—how silly. *Awfully* sorry. I must have got the wrong room,' said Janice, pink with embarrassment, backing away, and screwing her head round to look at the door.

'Hotel keys don't usually open more than one room,' Jeremy Fortescue pointed out. 'What number is your key?'

'Five-oh-nine. Look, there *must* be some mistake—'

'Must be. But why rush to correct it? You haven't told me your name.'

'Janice. Janice Fortescue.'

'Well, there you are.'

'Yes. I'm afraid so.'

'They thought you were my wife.'

'Yes.'

'At least you recognize me. That's half the battle. Now what will you have to drink?'

'No, really. I ought to tell them—'

'All the time in the world. Now what will it be? Gin and tonic? Vodka and lime?'

By this time he was very close to her. Closer than she would have liked. Or, to put it more accurately, too close for comfort. It was, really, a very exciting body: the shoulders certainly were broad, the chest wonderfully hairy, and the whole splendidly brown for an English April. And if his manner was the cheap seducer's (she told herself determinedly, though in fact she had known very few cheap seducers), still it was tense, nervous—almost neurotic in its intensity, which made her think of herself as a *need*, rather than as a victim. His face, close to, was haggard, the eyes almost rimmed. His hands were not exactly shaking, yet they were not still either—that might be incipient alcoholism, of course, but there was little alcohol on his breath. He behaved like a man who had just been through a shattering experience, or perhaps was just anticipating one. It was all, altogether, wonderfully . . . exciting.

'Perhaps just a small sherry,' Janice said.

Quite a while later, when Janice had not yet fallen, but was quite determined that she would fall (they were sprawled across the mock Louis Seize sofa, and she was speaking into more chest hair than she would have believed possible), she said:

'I have a confession to make.'

'Don't bother. This isn't the first time that's been done to me, don't you worry. However you fixed it, it was Lady Luck pulled the strings. You are but *exactly* my type. The fair hair, the snub nose—just what I always go for.'

'I did *not* fix it! That's a disgraceful suggestion!' Janice was as indignant about the crumby 'Lady Luck' line as about the suggestion. 'If you thought that surprise as I came in was acting, then you must be beyond recognizing genuine emotions. But I did say to reception that I was Mrs Jeremy Fortescue. I find it gets me better service. Besides, it *is* my real name.'

'It's not mine.'

'But of course it is. That's why I—'

'Do you know how I got it?'

He had pulled himself almost upright, and he sat over her, looking straight at her, and still speaking with that nervous intensity which she found so exciting and disturbing. It's that nervousness that gives him his appeal, his irresistibility, she said to herself. It's almost as if he had never . . .

'I was sixteen,' he said, in dark, reminiscent mood. 'Sixteen, going on seventeen. I'd just been expelled from my third school. Portlington. You had to be really appalling to be expelled from Portlington. I was the first since the First World War. Those were the days when girls still had unwanted pregnancies, of course. Now it would have been easily arranged. Anyway, I was desperate to go on the stage, or into films, or failing that, join the army or the Foreign Legion, or whatever. And my father took me to this provincial dump, not far from here, actually . . . what was the name? Bridgehead, that's it . . . he took me to Bridgehead, and he dragged me along to this school—the Drake School, Bridgehead, and a scummy little dump it was, and how they had the cheek to charge fees I don't know. Anyway, we were shown around, and given prospectuses, and a copy of the school magazine, and when we got back to the hotel my father said this was my last chance, but I was damned well going to work my guts out to make a go of it, or he'd want to know the reason why. He had the idea I ought to go to university. He was a very dim man, my father. Anyway, after dinner my father went down to the bar for a drink, and I was leafing through this damned school magazine, and I saw "Jeremy Fortescue—junior essay prize and under-15s hurdling cup"—'

Jeremy! Poor Jeremy! thought Janice, remembering the gold-stamped copy of *Hereward the Wake*, and the tiny silver-plated cup that was already showing the copper underneath the plate.

'—and I thought: that's a hell of a good name for an actor. It had an upper-class ring about it, but it left open the possibility of devilment. And I packed my things, hitch-hiked as far from Bridgehead as I could get, and eventually got taken on as ASM at a tiny rep theatre in Rotherham, run by a formidable lady who took a fancy to me. That was the beginning of it all . . .'

'Fascinating,' said Janice, as she felt his hand return to her shoulder. The hand, she noticed, was not quite still, but yet it showed a practised confidence, as well it might. Soon she was far beyond noticing whether it was still or not.

Some hours later, when the hotel was quiet, in the middle of a very dark night, Janice, more satisfied than she would have believed possible, heard Jeremy breathe in her ear: 'I always do it as if it were the last time.' Janice giggled and said:

'Do you know what my mother calls you?'

'I can imagine.'

'A fornicator, a child-molester and a drunkard.'

'She was fourteen, but she looked twenty-one,' said Jeremy Fortescue. 'Anyway, she did when I'd finished with her.'

'I notice you don't deny the rest.'

'How could I?' he asked, his breath now strong with whisky, and very close.

In the morning he insisted they have breakfast in his suite. When the waiter from the Prince Frederick dining-room brought it in, Janice was in the bathroom showering, but Jeremy shouted:

'Breakfast up, darling. But don't hurry.'

And Janice replied: 'Won't be a minute.'

They ate companionably, Jeremy seeming not to have eaten for hours. When they left, Jeremy brought the car round, and paid his bill with a credit card. He fetched Janice, and they sailed together through the foyer—how *lucky* she had had with her that enormous hat! she could not have looked anyone in the face—and then out into the car. He dropped her at the station, and behind the car's smoked windscreen they kissed goodbye. Jeremy got out of the car as Janice disappeared through the arch into the darkness of the station, and waved and called goodbye. On the station forecourt he created a small sensation, and signed a few autographs.

Once inside the station, Janice telephoned to the chairman of the meeting ('I've suddenly got this *appalling* headache'), and then took the next train home. Jeremy tore himself away from his little knot of fans, and drove straight to Markham studios, where he was due to begin work on an American adaptation of *The Last Days of Pompeii*. He looked marvellous in a toga, and he struck up an immediate rapport with the actress playing Nydia. From that first day they were inseparable, and the rest of the unit commented on it. 'Jeremy usually plays it so casual,' said one of those who'd worked with him before. 'Like he was one of nature's loners. Not this time.' One or two of them who were really friends of his added: 'Perhaps she's the one who'll finally get him away from that bitch.' The remark got around the studio, and was taken up even by those who did not know Jeremy Fortescue's wife. They were saying it when her body was found, six days later.

When the policeman came to the Prince Frederick, the clerk at Reception had been expecting him for some time, and was quite twittery with excitement. He had read of the death of Mrs Jeremy Fortescue in the papers, naturally, and had begun to think of himself as one of the last to see the dead woman alive. He even had a bookmark in the register, to show the Inspector where Jeremy Fortescue had signed in.

'But it's Mrs Fortescue we're interested in,' said the Inspector. 'You're quite sure she was with him?'

'Not with him. She came later. But I saw her—oh, definitely I saw her. I was on the desk here when she arrived.'

'She didn't sign the register?'

'Of course not. Her husband had already signed.'

'You've seen pictures of Mrs Fortescue?'

'Oh yes. In the newspapers. They weren't *good*, but I recognized them: the hair, that nose. Of course, I saw her only briefly, and one of the things that *is* impressed on us here is that we mustn't *stare* at the clientele: now and again someone may be with someone who—how shall I put it? he isn't legally married to. But that was Mrs Fortescue all right.' He permitted himself the vulgarity of leaning over the desk and asking breathlessly: 'Why?'

The Inspector was forthcoming. The newspapers that morning had mostly got the story right anyway, so there could be no harm in confirming them.

'Well, as you know—as everybody knows—she was murdered. Very possibly by a sex-maniac—we don't rule that out. Perhaps some casual pick-up. Perhaps by one or other of her regular boyfriends. She was by all accounts a very fascinating woman.'

A faint shadow of doubt wafted through the clerk's mind: the lady had not struck *him* as a very fascinating woman. But the doubt never got to his face, and the Inspector went on:

'That's why we have to eliminate the husband. There are some things about the death that make it look like a sudden fit of passion, in other words a quite unpremeditated murder. Fortescue and his wife had led a cat and dog existence for some time. The marriage was on, it was off—you know the kind of thing. People in the acting world seem to have different standards of morality in most respects. She'd certainly had plenty of affairs—'

'Not to mention him—'

'Precisely. But she kept, apparently, drawing him back. Or so his friends say. Expressing indifference about his affairs, but tormenting him about her own. Now, as you know, I imagine, the body was found buried in a coppice on Bromlet Heath, but it had been taken there, so we think. We can't be exact about the time of death, but the pathologist is pretty definite that he wouldn't expect it to be more than six days dead when it was found. And he'd say it in court. That puts her death, at the earliest, some time on Wednesday of last week. The lady, by the way, was renting a cottage twenty miles from here—rather remote, and nobody saw any comings or goings, and she had no contact to speak of with any of the neighbours.'

'A loner too?'

'Well, no. But not neighbourly. That explains why she

could have disappeared for several days without anybody noticing. Jeremy Fortescue says he wasn't expected at the cottage, and he didn't go there, and we have no evidence to contradict him. Says he isn't the cottage type, but the hotel type. His lifestyle would seem to bear *that* out. Now, the problem is that Wednesday, which is a sort of outer limit, according to the pathologist. She couldn't have been killed earlier than that. But if you say she spent Wednesday night here—'

'Oh, she did. Spent the night. Breakfast in their rooms. Went through this foyer. There's people in town—I've heard them talking in the bar—saw him seeing her off at the station.'

'Exactly. That's what we heard. And what he told us. Said he'd no idea where his wife was going. Said she was "her own woman". Well that would be Thursday morning. And since then Jeremy Fortescue has been absolutely tied up. Filming twelve or fifteen hours a day, and—well, let's call it vouched for at night. Markham Studios are a good thirty miles from Bromlet Heath, so to murder her, take her body there, and bury it, he'd need a good deal of time unvouched for, and he just hasn't got it. When they're working intensively on a film they're hardly alone for a minute, and he's been working—or whatever—practically non-stop.'

'I see.'

'For him to have done it, it would have to have been on the Wednesday.'

'Then really, it doesn't look as if it could have been him, does it, Inspector? And I must say, while he was here, he always behaved like a *perfect* gentleman.'

'Yes, clearly we're going to have to look elsewhere,' said the Inspector, with a shade of regret in his voice, for a domestic murder was always straightforward, whereas sex maniacs were the very devil to bring down.

*

Over the years, Janice Fortescue put the other Jeremy out of her mind, though it was difficult. Very difficult at first. All the time she was expecting something to blow her world apart. It quite put her off her tennis. When the news broke of Veronica Fortescue's death she was hour by hour expecting a visit from the police. Only when weeks went by and they hadn't come did she begin to gain a sense of renewed security. Only then could she bear to read the accounts of the case which she had stored up ('Your name-sake, darling,' she had explained to her Jeremy), and to order in her mind what must have happened.

The birth of her little boy was a great joy. He had a thick mop of black hair, even at birth, and as he grew up Jeremy, her Jeremy, used to say (how she wished he wouldn't): 'I don't know where my lad got that thick black hair from, because we're both so fair—and thin and sparse with it.' Jeremy adored the determined little boy, and often said: 'He's not going to spend his life in boring old insurance. You can see he hasn't the temperament for it.'

The name of the other Jeremy Fortescue often came up. He married again, he was nominated for an Oscar, he was arrested for brawling and breaking up a bar in Scotland somewhere. He seemed, still, to carry danger around with him. And of course in the Fortescue home the name was something of a joke, as it always had been. It came up when Janice's mother came to dinner with them, on their tenth wedding anniversary. She was a decidedly elderly lady now, and reminiscent, and after they had toasted the marriage and were waiting for the lady help (hired specially) to announce dinner, Janice's mother said:

'*What* a happy and successful marriage it has been! And to think I was so shocked when Janice told me about the engagement. What was it I called that other wretched Jeremy Fortescue? A fornicator, a child-molester and a drunkard!'

'And a murderer,' added Janice silently, hugging to herself her strong-willed, hairy child.

SISTERS

The light burned late that evening in Virginia McBride's office on the sixth floor. The Humanities Building was set apart from the other blocks—from Administration, from Physics, from the Social Sciences. It was surrounded by walkways and casual trees and shrubs, as if the humanities were delicate plants, to be sheltered and cosseted. So the light could be seen from the rest of the University, a pilot beacon surrounded by pitch blackness. Not that anyone much was around to notice. People mostly went home at five at the University of Borrowdale, West Dakota. And the light in Virginia McBride's office often burned late.

Virginia drew a firm line under the last words she had written, and screwed a half-smoked cigarette to extinction in her already overflowing ashtray. Finished. Ready for delivery tomorrow, at the Conference. Virginia liked giving reports to large assemblies, liked hearing her clear, forceful, indignant voice ringing round a hall, liked seeing the rows on rows of passionate female faces gazing up at her. The Ninth National Delegate Conference on Women's History, to be held in Chicago, would be the high-spot of her year, the largest, most prestigious assembly she would address.

The discovery of Women's History had been a godsend to Virginia. Till then she had toiled in the doldrums of trade statistics from nineteenth-century Boston, though in the 'sixties she had dabbled in Black Studies and even taught a couple of courses, *faute de nègres*. But this was something much more exciting. Here was a whole new area—half the population ignored by historians, slighted by contemporary chroniclers—and one in which she suffered none of the humiliating disabilities which compromised her usefulness in the field of Black Studies. So untapped was this field, so sparse the information on even quite important aspects of it, that it left infinite room for conjecture, wild assertion, unbridled indignation.

Virginia thrived on indignation. She organized it. She got together little groups, merged them into larger groups, and orchestrated their indignations. Feminism was essentially, for her, a Trade Union of professional women advancing their own and each other's careers. She got scholarships and grants for her friends and disciples, and they got Visiting Professorships and distinguished guest lecturing spots for her.

Luckily the kids had left home early. The youngest, Alexander, had been shipped back East to his father after that unfortunate letter to the local paper. Then she'd been alone, free to pursue her professional career, free to pursue the various causes that made demands on her leisure time —the Pressure for Equal Standing group, for example, which had among other worthy trail-blazing enterprises brought such effective pressure to bear on the local symphony orchestra to give equal time to women composers that they had revolutionized its concert programme, and emptied the concert hall. Virginia, hating to be closed in, opened the window of her office and gazed out over the campus, her church and her battleground, with a grim smile on her face. Yes, life was full for Virginia.

The light burned late, too, in the secretaries' office on the other side of the Humanities Building. Susan Cox sat behind a spectacularly clean desk and talked into the phone.

'What am I doing? Twiddling my thumbs, that's what I'm doing. My desk is so hygienic you could eat off it. All I'm doing is sitting around waiting for this report that's got to be typed . . . Yes, I'll see you at eight-thirty. Nothing's going to keep me away. I'm really looking forward to the party afterwards—great that it's Saturday tomorrow . . . Just get Madam Associate Professor McBride's report typed and I'll be off home to change . . . Hey, I think that's her.'

And she banged down the phone and sat by her pristine desk, the typewriter uncovered, ready for action.

Virginia McBride came swinging into the room, all sensible suit and sensible shoes, all short hair-do and thick-rimmed glasses. Well preserved she was, like a pickled damson. Could easily be a no-nonsense thirty-five, though in fact she was ten years older than that.

'Here it is,' she said, slapping a sheaf of papers down on the desk. 'I'll pick it up for proof-reading in an hour.'

Susan picked up the sheaf and cleared her throat at the departing square-set back.

'Er, Professor McBride . . .'

'Yes?'

'I'm afraid I shan't be able to get this finished tonight.' Virginia swung round, but Susan held her ground, leafing through the wodge of paper. 'There must be fifteen pages or more to type here. I have to be gone by seven-thirty—seven forty-five at the very latest. Of course I'll do as much as I can.'

Virginia McBride looked at her steadily.

'I don't think you quite understand the position, Miss Cox,' she said, her voice slightly raised, as if talking to a backward child. 'Professor Lindgren must have explained to you that someone had to be here this evening to type my report for Chicago.'

'Professor Lindgren *asked* one of us to stay back to type it. All the others said no. I said I'd stay till seven-thirty. I have plans for the rest of the evening.'

'Then I'm afraid you'll just have to revise your plans.'

'I'm afraid I can't do that, Professor McBride.'

Virginia McBride came back towards the desk and bared her teeth in an alligator smile.

'You need this job, don't you, Susan?'

Susan Cox flinched at the Christian name. Christian names always went with threats for Virginia McBride. But, oh yes, in her position she needed the job. And Virginia McBride had Professor Lindgren well and truly under her thumb.

'I like it here,' said Susan cautiously.

'Well then,' said Virginia, the smile widening still more ferociously. 'I suggest you get down to that report.'

'Professor McBride, I have a date at eight-thirty.'

'Then you'll just have to cancel it, won't you, Susan?'

Virginia McBride closed the door of the secretaries' office firmly behind her and marched down the corridor. Susan Cox had already been put completely out of her mind. It was Virginia's great strength that she could concentrate totally on the matter in hand, ignore side issues. There was to be an evening meeting tomorrow in Chicago after the main session—an exclusive, ticket-only, gin-and-tonic affair where many of her ex-students, colleagues and professional cronies would be getting together for self-help and mutual congratulation. They would certainly expect a little impromptu address from her. Something inspirational.

'The history of women which we here are beginning to write,' she improvised to herself, 'is one of suppression, of a domination authorized by State and Church, and more terrible in its effects than any of the right- and left-wing tyrannies we have known in our lifetime. The denial to women of an independent existence, the untrammelled assertion of male authority, the suppression of all feelings of sisterhood in that half of the pop—'

She clicked her tongue with annoyance. The cleaner had gone into her room and was busy with bucket and mop.

'I'm afraid I'm still working here,' she said, walking in over the wet floor.

'Won't be a minute,' said Mrs Makowski, mopping up.

'I'm sorry, you'll have to come back later,' said Virginia, sitting down at her desk and opening up a new packet of cigarettes.

'This is the last office on the sixth,' said Mrs Makowski, her hands on her sturdy peasant hips. 'If I go down to the fifth this one won't be cleaned till Monday night.'

'I shall most certainly expect to find it clean when I get in Monday morning,' said Virginia, calmly settling down to make some notes for her impromptu address. 'If it weren't, I would naturally send a note to Administration. It's up to you, isn't it?'

Mrs Makowski bit her lips, as if sewing them together to prevent words escaping, but she went out into the corridor.

'Darling, I know. Do you think I'm not mad too? But so long as I want this job that bitch has the upper hand.'

Susan wondered whether her boyfriend would propose on the spot: would say 'Chuck up the job and marry me.' She was a divorcee of twenty-eight, living with her mother and a daughter of three. Life wasn't easy. If he proposed, would she accept? Simon was an artist. He had a gallery showing tonight and a party afterwards. She'd been looking forward to it for weeks. And quite apart from that, she'd be letting him down.

Simon did not propose.

'Look, I'll be there for the party,' Susan said, relying on her power to soothe him down once she was there. 'The quicker I'm through with this, the sooner I get there.'

She put down the receiver and went back to her manuscript. Virginia's writing was a mess. What was this? 'Women are beginning to seige—' no—'seize the opportunities . . .'

Some women, thought Susan bitterly.

Virginia McBride went down to the Common Room on the fifth floor to make herself a cup of coffee. Luckily the kettle was on and steaming, so she poured it over the instant coffee in her cup and sat at one of the tables skimming through the local paper. She had stopped taking it since her son had written that protest letter about how children were used as unpaid domestic slaves. Another of the cleaners came in, Mrs O'Hare, a fat old thing with a foul Irish temper. She took the lid off the kettle and peered inside.

'Here, that was for my cup of tea,' she said.

'Plenty more water in the tap,' said Virginia, and she crumpled up the paper and went along to the office.

'I'll proof-read what you've done,' she said, taking up the crisp white sheets. 'That will save time and suit us both, won't it, Susan?'

She showed her fillings again and sat informally on a table. Susan Cox went on typing. My God, what a slave-driver, she thought. No wonder your bloody children fled the nest. If that letter in the paper was anything to go by, they were nothing but unpaid labour. More like the cotton plantations of old Virginia than a home.

'Well, the first page will have to be done again, for a start,' said Virginia, coolly swinging her heels as she read on.

Susan typed a whole line in capitals.

At a quarter to nine it was at last finished. Virginia took her script up to her room, closed the window, put her coat around her shoulders, locked her office door and marched along the grey linoleumed corridor floor. Home, bath, straight to bed, with the alarm to wake her at three. What a time to catch a plane! Still, Virginia prided herself on her ability to keep up with a demanding schedule. A Professional Woman had to be able to, in this day and age. She walked towards the stairs, then changed her mind and went to the lift. It was an awful lift. Virginia hated enclosed spaces of any kind, and if someone pressed the button for this one just before it got to the third floor it jammed. In the daytime she would never take it, but luckily it was evening, and nobody much was about. It would save a few minutes. Virginia walked into the lift.

*

Mrs Makowski and Mrs O'Hare stood jawing by the lift as Susan Cox came out of the office and locked it.

'Through at last?' they asked sympathetically. 'She ought to be skinned alive, that one.'

'I've missed the showing,' said Susan miserably. 'My boyfriend had a showing of his pictures, and I've missed it. The party doesn't start till ten. I suppose I'll just go home and put my glad rags on. I feel like death.'

The lift light showed at the sixth floor, and the machinery began making little coughing noises, preparatory to starting. As it descended, Virginia McBride saw through the slit in the door the three women around the lift shaft, and they saw her. On an impulse Mrs O'Hare strode forward and, judging her moment precisely, pressed the button just as the lift was approaching the third floor. They heard it stop suddenly with a jerk.

'Oh my God!' said Susan. 'You shouldn't have done that. She gets claustrophobia.'

'I know,' said Mrs O'Hare.

Little stuttering noises came from the lift shaft.

'She's pressing the emergency button,' said Mrs Makowski.

'She treats me like dirt,' said Susan from nothing. 'And I am not dirt.'

'We're none of us her dirt,' said Mrs O'Hare. 'The caretaker's off sick until Monday.'

'She'll get hysterical,' said Susan. 'She always does, even if the building's full of people.'

To confirm her words, shouting started coming from the shaft.

'It's that claustrophobia thing,' said Mrs O'Hare, nodding her head grimly.

There came another shout, and another, then suddenly a howl, half human, grotesque, followed by another till it became continuous. The little shaft echoed with cries and sobs and moans, rising to a hideous intensity.

'Did you say till Monday?' asked Mrs Makowski.

'That's right,' said Mrs O'Hare. 'It's his arthritis. We're the last ones in the building.'

They stood around, the little group of women, listening to the animal sounds of terror and outrage coming from the lift shaft.

'I could do with a cup of tea,' said Mrs Makowski.

'Tea?' said Susan. 'That's an awfully typical women's drink, don't you think? I could do with something stronger.'

'She keeps a bottle of bourbon in her room,' said Mrs Makowski.

'Kept,' said Susan.

'Come on, sisters,' said Mrs Makowski, waving her skeleton key. 'Let's go have us a slug.'

THE INJURED PARTY

Derek Mattingley was unsure of the appropriate behaviour for a man whose ex-wife has just died. No doubt one of the with-it etiquette books had a section on it. Luckily mourning itself has practically passed away, so delicate questions of full or half-mourning did not present themselves. A sober suit was all that could be expected, and as a Lloyd's broker Derek wore a sober suit every day of his life. Similarly with his behaviour, which in working hours was habitually tinged with gravity, so that he had no difficulty in shaking his head sadly when anyone brought the subject up, or in offering remarks like: 'It's Gavin I feel sorry for: only two years married.' With closer friends he ventured: 'I often wondered whether she was entirely well when she was married to me.' Then he would dismiss the matter with another shake of the head: 'It's a sad business.'

Inwardly, of course, he was over the moon with delight.

He had been married to Anne-Marie for seven years. She had cooked well, both for him and for the little dinner-parties which Derek rather went in for. She had looked decorative at the cocktail-parties they regularly threw, had turned eyes in the stalls at Covent Garden, or at Chichester, where they sometimes drove to take in a play at festival time. Sometimes on holiday—Sardinia, as often as not, or the dear old South of France, which Derek always said you still couldn't beat —she had looked perfectly stunning. Derek regarded her as an undoubted asset.

Which had made her announcement that she was leaving him such a hideous blow. It was all so damned unexpected. She had said she was just an adjunct to his business career. Well, why hadn't she complained before? And why had she made no bones about living off the proceeds of that business

career? She said he had no interest in her as a person. Good
heavens, what nonsense! He'd married her, hadn't he? How
could she say he wasn't interested in her as a person?

But the worst was to come.

'Doesn't it mean anything,' he had demanded, 'that we've
had seven years together, day and night?'

'Are you referring to bed?' she had asked. 'Well, there
was never much of interest in *that* department, was
there?'

They were words from which Derek Mattingley flinched,
as if struck. What had been wrong with their sex? It had
seemed perfectly all right to him. What had she been expecting that he hadn't given her? And where had she formed
her standards of comparison?

Part of the answer to that last question soon became
obvious. She was leaving him, she said, for Gavin Hobhouse.

Derek really had to sit down and think who Gavin Hobhouse was. He barely knew the man, though it was true he
had been to dinner. That was when Derek had thought he
might be useful in the matter of National and Regional
shares, but he hadn't responded to his prompting—in fact,
he had hardly said a word all evening.

That, Anne-Marie said, was because they were already
going to bed together. Gavin was a man of old-fashioned
probity, of deeply conservative principles. He was embar-
rassed by the situation, and took refuge in taciturnity.

'The strong, silent type?' inquired Derek satirically.

'Well, yes, he is, rather. Strong, simple emotions.'

'His conservative principles didn't stop him breaking up
my hearth and home, did they?'

'The fire was *out*, the home was a shell,' said Anne-Marie.
'Otherwise I don't think he ever would have spoken.'

Gavin apparently was an ex-guardsman, but was now
something in the City, as Derek—when he had racked
his brains—knew. He was, from all he could learn,
just as Anne-Marie described him: simple, passionate,

old-fashioned in his morality, strict in his standards.
'She'd be well-advised not to play around while she's
married to *him*,' said one of Derek's friends in the City.
Then, with a sideways glance at Derek, he added: 'But
then, perhaps she won't want to.'

Before Derek shunted this particular stock-broker over to
his list of ex-friends, he asked casually:

'Jealous, would you say?'

'As a tiger, I'd guess. That's just an opinion, of course.
Until now he's never had anyone much to be jealous about.'

'Quite,' said Derek.

After the separation Derek rebuilt his life, or rather took
steps to ensure the smooth continuation of his old life in all
essentials. In some respects very little needed to be done.
The cleaning lady came in as before, and now and then left
him a cold meal, or something that could easily be heated
up in the oven. Mostly Derek ate out. The laundryman
called, and Derek did a large shop once a fortnight at the
local supermarket, just as he had in Anne-Marie's time. He
found a very reliable Algerian couple, students, who would
come in to cook for dinner-parties, or do the necessary at
any other drinks-and-chat gatherings Derek might arrange.
Life went on really very satisfactorily, except that sometimes
in the middle of the night he would awake sweating and
panting, and sometimes crying out with what he recognized
was rage. Luckily there was no one in the house to hear
him. He got into the habit, on these disturbing occasions,
of going straight to the bathroom and taking a shower. In
the mornings he was his usual cool self.

It was some time before he made any approach to Gavin
Hobhouse. To move too quickly would certainly arouse in
that conventional, simple soul either distaste or suspicion.
It would have, he knew, to be a fortuitous and spontaneous
coming together. What in fact happened was that one
lunch-time, in a City pub, Derek saw in the glass behind the bar that Gavin was standing by his shoulder

in the one o'clock scrum. Derek eased himself round.

'Hello, old chap,' he said. 'Too silly that we shouldn't talk, don't you think? Let me get you a drink.'

If Gavin Hobhouse had been what used to be called the injured party, it is likely that he would have rejected this advance. A situation where both men nodded frostily to each other when their paths happened to cross would clearly have been much more to his conventional taste. As the guilty party, however, it would certainly be churlish, not to say un-Christian, to reject the hand of friendship, or at least of reconciliation. He tried to keep the stiffness out of his voice when he said:

'Scotch and water, please.'

He backed his way out of the scrum, and got them a place by a little ledge on a far wall, and there he waited for Derek and for the inevitable conversation that must ensue without any obvious signs of distaste on his handsome face.

'How *is* Anne-Marie, anyway,' said Derek, coming back with the drinks.

'Oh, fine. She's fine,' said Gavin Hobhouse.

'Good. Good. You know, though I didn't think so at the time, I realize now that what happened was obviously the best thing in the long run. Common enough thing to happen, these days, after all—what? Easy to make a mistake in one's first marriage. Only sensible thing is to cut your losses and get out.'

It wasn't at all how Gavin Hobhouse viewed marriage, but in the circumstances he could only murmur, 'Right.' Derek, on this first meeting, wisely turned the talk to the current scandals in the banking world, and to the position of the Governor of the Bank of England in them. It was only as they were getting ready to go back to their respective offices that Derek, obliquely, returned to the personal matters that lay between them.

'Ever see anything of Anne-Marie's mother?' he asked, buttoning up the jacket of his pinstripe suit.

'Yes. Oh yes. We went up to stay at Penstone a couple of months ago.'

'Wonderful woman,' said Derek with enthusiasm. 'A real legend in her own lifetime.'

Anne-Marie's mother had had a raffish career, which had begun when she was a member of the Princess Margaret set back in the 'fifties, and which, apart from various flings, had brought her no fewer than four husbands. She was currently Lady Crawley, with a country seat and a national reputation.

'We always got on like a house on fire,' said Derek, as they threaded their way through the mob of City drinkers. 'You can see where Anne-Marie got her—charm.'

That evening, as he sat watching Channel 4 news and forked absent-mindedly into his mouth a shepherd's pie that his daily had left ready for him, his meditations added spice to the humdrum fare. Clearly he was not going to be able to talk to Gavin Hobhouse too often. Any suspicion that he was waylaying him, cultivating him in any way, would be counter-productive. Conversation between them had to be very occasional, and apparently as fortuitous as that first meeting had been. Derek decided that his first priority must be to find out what Gavin Hobhouse did in his lunch-hour. No doubt he had various haunts—pubs, cafés, restaurants —depending on the dictates of his digestion. He, Derek, went to a variety of places. He was quite willing to add to their number.

Thus he had waved across the room to Gavin in Alberto's in Curtin Street a couple of times before, three months after their first meeting, they actually were seated close enough to talk. By a combination of planning and good luck he turned into the little eating place just two minutes after Gavin, and found that the table next to his was the only one vacant. They greeted each other very much as two City gentlemen will, when they have a definite but limited acquaintanceship. They swapped odd remarks about the state of the economy and feeling in the CBI while Derek read the menu and ordered. They discovered (not very surprisingly, since Derek always winkled out Gavin's opinion first) that they felt pretty much the same about these topics. When Derek saw a couple standing waiting for a table he suggested that he move over to Gavin's—which was unusual, since he was neither generous by nature nor courteous, except within convention.

'Silly to take up two tables,' he said, moving his things over. 'It gets pretty crowded in here.'

'Yes, it does,' said Gavin, eating, perhaps, a shade faster.

'Used to go to the Coq d'Or at lunch-times—specially if Anne-Marie was up for the day. She loves French cooking, doesn't she? But either it's gone downhill, or it's not somewhere to go on your own. I prefer this place now.'

'Anne-Marie's more into English cooking at the moment,' said Gavin, apparently to keep the thing going.

'Really? *Really?* Not that she wasn't always perfectly good at the traditional English while we were married . . . I suppose that would be Cousin Simon's influence, wouldn't it?'

'Couldn't say. I believe she has had some recipes from him, yes. She's been talking about a book.'

'Oh, jolly good. I always said she ought to go into the cook-book business. See much of Simon, does she?'

'Oh yes, now and again. He comes over to us, or she goes over to him.'

'They're practically brother and sister, aren't they? Naturally, since they were brought up together. I used to think that if mother-in-law hadn't dumped Anne-Marie on to her sister during one of her grand passions, those two would probably have got married. I *like* Simon, though, don't you?'

'Yes, very much . . . Though I haven't seen much of him.'

'Some don't, you know—like him, I mean. It's that golden boy air he has about him. That look of being the

Rupert Brooke *de nos jours*. That air of playing gentlemanly cricket on the green, taking crumpets at the vicarage, with croquet afterwards in the dusk, that feeling that there must be some elderly novelist somewhere sighing after him and writing him passionate little notes. I always have that feeling about Simon, don't you?'

Gavin left a moment's silence.

'Well, no—I hadn't thought of him quite like that.'

'Sorry. Was I being too ridiculously fanciful? Well, certainly one thing we never would have predicted for him would be that he would end up owning and running a restaurant, even one as special as the Old Watermill. Awfully useful for Anne-Marie, anyway, if he supplies her with recipes. I'm glad she's seeing a lot of him. She probably gives him some kind of stable base. I think that's what he needed during all this racketing around he used to do.'

'Well, er—we'll hope so.'

'Yes, it *is* difficult to think of Anne-Marie as a stable base, isn't it?' said Derek, with a light-hearted laugh. 'But I think you may well find that that's how it works itself out, with those two.'

He looked guilelessly into Gavin Hobhouse's face with its faint, bewildered frown.

Derek was gratified that the next time he and Gavin talked, it was Gavin who made the approach. They were at one of these launching parties for something financial, an early-evening affair to which Gavin had brought Anne-Marie. Derek and his ex-wife kissed and exchanged inanities, and then went their separate ways. Normally Derek would have downed a couple of drinks and then made off, for these were not the sort of functions that anyone but an incurable soak would stay at for long. But almost from the beginning he felt that Gavin's eyes were on him, whatever their respective positions in the room, and whoever they were talking to. Before long he made an excuse to the incredibly boring City type with whom he had been making incredibly boring conversation, and went over to the table of incredibly boring light refreshments. He was helping himself to a triangle of bread with cream cheese and chopped ham on top when a shadow across the light made him realize that Gavin was at his elbow.

Gavin, when he *did* talk about personal matters, came to them at once.

'I say, Derek, I wonder if I could ask you something?'

'Yes, of course, old chap. So long as I'm not bound to silence by company policy . . .'

'Oh, it's not professional. It's—well, I wondered if Anne-Marie and Simon saw a lot of each other while you were married.'

Derek put down his savoury and turned to face Gavin with an expression of great concern on his face.

'Oh, I say, old chap—really, I blame myself for this. No, really. I never dreamed . . . I can see what has happened. I've been putting silly ideas into your head.'

'No, it's just—'

'Yes, I have. I can see it. Well, just don't think any more about it. You've got hold of the wrong end of the stick entirely.'

'Yes, but did she?'

'Yes, of course she did. And she'll go on seeing him frequently till the end of her days, unless they have some kind of lo—of family tiff. They're bound up with each other, always have been since they were children. But there's nothing *in* it, nothing of the sort that you've been imagining.'

Gavin stood silent for a moment, then muttered:

'She certainly does see a lot of him.'

'Of course she does. But you know what an open-hearted girl she is. When she gives, she gives entirely. I mean, look at her now—'

He waved his hand to the far corner of the room. Anne-Marie was standing with a man, he stiff-backed and fair-haired, she with her face close to his, for she was short-sighted, looking up intently, laughing at his jokes, giving him the feeling that he was, for that moment, the only man she cared about in the world. Stupid bitch, thought Derek, a spurt of venom seeming to shoot through his veins. You're bringing it on yourself, you silly tart.

'I mean, look at her. Look at the way she gives her all to anyone she happens to talk to. It's in the blood. Part of her mother's technique, if you ask me. But in her case it doesn't *mean* anything. She's giving him the idea that the sun shines out of his anus, but she probably doesn't know the man from Adam.'

'Actually, that's Bruno Kohl,' said Gavin stiffly. 'Friend of the family.'

'There you *are*, you see. Friend of the family. But if you just *saw* them together, in the abstract, so to speak, you'd think—putting the thing bluntly—there was something between them. And with Simon there is the added thing that he is practically a brother to her. Remember how often she was ill in childhood, those long periods when she was laid up with that dicky heart of hers. She relied on him for companionship. It's not surprising that they got into the habit of depending on one another.'

'No,' said Gavin, but after a pause.

'So put the thing clean out of your mind. Good Lord, it's awful to see a happily married chap like you entertaining ideas of that kind. Forget about it entirely.'

But Gavin, fortunately, could not do that. The thing about people with few, simple ideas is that the ideas tend to take them over entirely. And the fact was that, as far as Gavin's Victorian ideas about faithfulness and marital exclusivity were concerned, he had violated them by taking Anne-Marie from Derek in the first place. Or Anne-Marie, in particular, had violated them, with his connivance.

Now Derek and Gavin found that they met fairly frequently at lunch-time. At every meeting Derek noticed with satisfaction fresh care-lines round the eyes, along the

forehead. Even the eyes wandered insecurely around the
room, and the mouth seemed slacker. Every time they met,
the subject of Anne-Marie hung in the air from the first
moment, and every time it in the end came up—was brought
up by Gavin. For one or two meetings, Derek kept up the
notion that he was quite sure there was nothing in Gavin's
suspicions. This was the easier to do because he was in fact
sure that, whatever her relations with other men had been,
her love for Simon her cousin was child-like and sisterly.
Gradually, though, responding to Gavin's insistent suspicion, he shifted to a new tack, so that before long the
suspicion was accepted between them as fact.

'It's a funny family,' Derek would say. 'I yield to no one
in my admiration for Lady Crawley. Still, that doesn't mean
I'd want to have been one of her four.'

Before long that became: 'You can't wonder Anne-Marie
is as she is.'

Quite soon Gavin's watchful eye, ever active at parties,
dinners and other social occasions, would detect other men
who he was convinced were enjoying Anne-Marie's favours.
He would ring home during the day and be distraught if he
found his wife not at home, or would detect suspicious
noises if she was there. Derek, on their meetings, would be
reassuring.

'I'm sure it's more a matter of *manner*, rather than there
being anything much going *on*.'

Eventually Gavin would cry: 'Of course there's something
going on. I see how she behaves with these men, don't I?'

'I didn't say there was nothing going on. After all, she
deceived me with you, didn't she? I just mean it's not all
that *serious*. You've got to learn to take these things a bit
more easily, old man. Be relaxed about the whole thing.
Because there's nothing going to change her now.'

The last time Gavin and Derek met, Anne-Marie's prom-
iscuity was by now an established fact for both of them.

'I can see it bothers you, old man,' said Derek, digging

into his sorbet, 'but you've got to face it, we're living in the twentieth century. All the old standards have gone by the board long ago. And, after all, you've still got the major shareholding in her.'

'God!' said Gavin, spitting the word out.

'I wouldn't mind betting she still loves you. That's how you must see it. It's something in her nature that makes her as she is, but basically she still loves you, in her way. It wasn't like that with us.'

'What do you mean?'

'I mean, when we were married and she was playing around—and my God, did she play around!—our marriage was already dead for her. Trouble was, it wasn't dead for me. Though, God knows, I sometimes *wanted* her dead. Funny to think back on it now, but I did. Desperately. Thought of going out and picking the good old foxglove leaves . . .'

'Foxglove leaves?'

'Digitalis. Good for the heart in small quantities, fatal for someone like Anne-Marie if she had a hefty dose of it. That was the sort of silly idea I played with, so you can see I've been through it too. But in the end you shake down into the situation. Take the line of "least said, soonest mended." In the end, whatever she gets up to is so much water off a duck's back. You'll see, that's how it will be with you.'

Derek first knew for sure that that was *not* how it was to be with Gavin when he heard of Anne-Marie's death. Ironically, it was her cousin Simon who telephoned him to tell him.

'I suppose it was always in the cards, with that heart of hers,' Derek said to him. 'Awful for *you*—you two were always so close. And I don't mind telling you, it's a shock for me too, in spite of it all.'

That was early on in the morning, about nine, before he took off for the City. Throughout the day there was a trickle of people who had heard, made the connection, and murmured sympathy. Even in the pub that night someone had heard, and the word went round. Derek downed a couple of shorts, then left. There was a lot of sympathy for him in the Saloon Bar: it had hit him hard, they said. When he got home he wondered whether to ring up then. He thought about it for a bit, then decided it would look better if he had slept on it first.

So in fact it was next morning, after breakfast, when he rang up the police and said:

'Look, I know I'm probably being silly, but you see my ex-wife has died, and quite by chance I was talking to her husband one lunch-time a few days ago—he's been having trouble with her, as I did—and I made this silly remark about digitalis . . . Yes, digitalis. I'm quite sure there's nothing in it, but it's been nagging at me since I heard she'd died, and I find I can't get it out of my head. What do you think? *Should* you look into it a bit?'

JUST ANOTHER KIDNAP

The kidnap went badly almost from the first. At five minutes past eleven Arrigo Furlani (manager of the Banco Nazionale Piemontese, and treasurer of the Rome branch of the Christian Democratic party) stepped out of the portals of the Bank's headquarters in Via Sparafucile, Rome. He was gesturing angrily with his one free hand (an Italian with a briefcase is a man half-crippled) and sending a machine-gun rattle of orders and expostulations in the direction of his obsequious underlings in the shadow of the portals.

'*Presto! Presto! Via!*' he concluded, half-turning in their direction as he surged ahead, and barging oblivious through the paths of passers-by. He did not see the dirty blue Fiat parked near his own Mercedes, nor did he heed the presence of the leather-jacketed young men some yards away on the pavement, who were observing his departure from the corners of their dark eyes.

The seizure was the work of a moment. A burst of machine-gun fire killed the chauffeur, and then the young man holding the gun turned it inwards and sprayed the doorway of the Banco Nazionale as a warning. None of the obsequious underlings showed sign of wanting to fight the thing through. Arrigo Furlani found a gag in his mouth and his hands handcuffed behind his back. In the scuffle to get him into the waiting Fiat he dropped his briefcase, and in seconds he was in the front seat and the car was beginning to career off eastwards down Via Sparafucile.

It was then that things began to go wrong. As the seizer of Furlani tore open the back door of the Fiat a shot rang out from the west end of the street. He fell at once. The two other gunmen, who had nearly gained their own car, which they were to drive in the other direction, looked round as they dived into it, and it was the last thing they did. As the dirty Fiat swerved on two wheels into Viale Mascagni the bullets took over around the headquarters of the Banco Nazionale, leaving a spectacle of leaking petrol tanks, broken glass and spilt blood. To the dead chauffeur were added the bodies of the three members of the Red League, sprawled in melodramatic attitudes of abandonment around the middle of Via Sparafucile. Three for one: it seemed a reasonable proportion. Before long the newspaper boys would be calling it a triumph for the carabinieri.

Mario Galbani, sweating profusely, drove like a maniac with one hand on the wheel up Viale Mascagni. In front, around and behind were other people driving like maniacs with one hand on the wheel. The back door, left open as his companion fell to the first bullet, had shut itself during the perilous two-wheel turn into Viale Mascagni. There was nothing to mark his car off from the other Rome motorists. No one paid any attention to him, or if they did, and connected him with the gunfire that was still to be heard in the distance, they made sure that their attention would not be too obvious.

'Just another kidnap,' said a good Roman citizen to his wife, and edged himself into the furthest lane.

Mario's free hand held the gun, which had been poked unnervingly into Arrigo Furlani's side from the moment he was dumped in the passenger seat. Furlani had his eyes open, and was making convulsive movements with his mouth around the gag. Mario kept his foot on the accelerator as they neared the end of Viale Mascagni. Left, then right, then right again. They'd drummed it into him so many times. Why in God's name had he been chosen to drive? He, who'd only been three times in Rome. Why, in the name of Jesus, he had asked? Because you're too stupid to shoot anyone, they had replied. And who the hell is this Jesus you keep talking about?

Left, on two wheels, with shrieking brakes, into the Via Mastromiei, the sweat pouring down his face like Alpine streams in springtime. Left, then right. Right into Viale Corbaccio, keeping with the stream of traffic, but keeping ahead of the crowd. Left, then right, then—left again, wasn't it? As he swerved left and saw with horror a tide of advancing traffic he imagined—surely it must have been imagination? —a muffled voice from the seat beside him:

'Turn right, you idiot.'

With a soprano screech of brakes Mario swerved the car around and, careering wildly, continued the progress out of Rome.

It was a two-and-a-half-hour drive before they would get there, and long before that Mario decided he was going mad with tension and frustration. His gun hand went to sleep. Cautiously he transferred the weapon to his right hand, and drove with his left. As they emerged from the city into the Campagna he stole glances at his companion. The glances were returned—operatically, contemptuously. The sun beat down on them. Mario wiped his brow with his free hand, and the Fiat swerved unnervingly towards the ditch. Peremptory cursings came from behind the gag. Mario would have liked to open the window, but he didn't quite dare to let go of the wheel for that long. They careered along at 130, like any Italian family out for a day at the coast.

By midday the sun was unbearable. Mario was dying for a drink. Typical of his friends, Mario thought, that they'd spent last night reading *On the Condition of the Working Classes in England*, and hadn't even thought to buy in a few bottles of Coke. 'Maniacs,' he muttered. Then, wondering about their fate, he crossed himself. The car swerved madly towards the ditch again.

It was nearly three by the time they arrived at the ruined castle of Orvino-Montevedere. Never much of a castle, it had been abandoned not long after the Risorgimento by its family (which was not much of a family either, and had later sunk to being pork butchers in a suburb of Naples). Now it was a three-storey ruin, with collapsed roof, holes for windows, and a ridiculous tower which nobody but a fool would ascend. The road to it was hardly more than a path. But at least the members of the Red League (Orvino-Montevedere branch) had thought to remove the worst of the boulders. Mario did not slacken speed until he drove into the dusty circle which served as a courtyard. Then he came to a halt in an anguished scream of brakes.

'Get out,' he squeaked threateningly, his gun still pointed.

'Mmmm—nnn—ttt—' spluttered Arrigo Furlani.

Mario had to admit that he had a point. With his hands handcuffed behind him, Furlani was in no condition to let himself out. His gun still pointed nervously at the passenger seat, Mario got out, went round the back, and opened the right side door. Almost as if he were Furlani's chauffeur.

'In there,' he shouted uncertainly. 'Pig.'

He waved his gun towards the Grand (and crumbling) Entrance. Stiff with the discomfort of a long journey with his hands behind him, Furlani stumbled forward. They came into the high, dark hall. At least here there was some shade from the appalling sun.

'Up!' shouted Mario, his voice now having sunk to its usual tenor. 'Up, capitalist leech!'

Furlani looked at the rickety stairs and turned to expostulate. Mario, his hand trembling, pointed his gun at the banker's substantial gut. Furlani turned and stumbled up the stairs. Straight ahead of them on the first floor was a large room, perhaps in palmier days the seignorial bedroom.

'Forward, lackey of bourgeois democracy!' cried Mario, his relief at the end of his ordeal making him a touch more confident. 'Sit! On that chair!'

And so their journey ended. The handcuffs were removed, and Mario tied Furlani's chest and shoulders, and then his ankles, to the chair. Then at last he could throw away his gun.

Oh yes, but there was one more thing. The comrades had insisted upon it. Mari turned to his captive.

'Comrade Furlani,' he proclaimed, his voice going skywards again at the unusualness of the task, 'you are a prisoner of the Red League, a captive of the people, and your seizure is a just expression of the anger of the proletariat at their exploitation at the hands of the international fascist-capitalist clique. You will be tried by a people's court, at which you will be allowed every opportunity to speak in your own defence. When you have been found guilty you will be shot by democratically-chosen representatives of the people. If, however, you repent of your acts of oppression against the working class, and if—if . . .' What came next?

'If a ransom is paid, I suppose,' came spluttering from behind the gag.

'Yes—and if a ransom is paid, the sum to be decided by an *ad hoc* general assembly of the Red League, Orvino-Montevedere branch, you may after a period of political re-education be regarded as having served exemplary punishment, and you will, subject to certain conditions, be set free.'

Marco finished and wiped his brow.

'Bravo!' came the muffled voice.

'What,' asked Arrigo Furlani, 'are we waiting for?'

His gag had been removed, because Mario was tired of asking him to repeat everything. His voice was dry, crackling, satirical.

'My friends,' said Mario. 'We await my friends.'

'Your friends,' said Arrigo Furlani, 'are either under arrest or dead. Remembering the bullets as we drove off, probably the latter. Even the carabinieri do not miss when they use so many.'

'*Dio mio*,' said Mario, in whom a religious upbringing died hard. '*Povero Aldo. Povero Gianni. Pover*—'

'Yes, yes. You're not saying your rosary. Why don't you turn on the television and see?'

Mario had forgotten the little battery television set they had rented two days before in Naples, procured especially (for television was a bourgeois palliative to divert the attention of the working class from their just anger and demands) to follow the reactions of the ruling cadres to the kidnapping, and to judge their intentions as to the ransom demands. Mario looked at the set, and walked uncertainly towards it.

'The button on the right,' snapped the captive.

The set sprang to life, with gay bandstand music. It was a cartoon.

'Splendid!' said Furlani bitterly. 'I get kidnapped, and all Italy goes on watching Mr Magoo.'

Mario sat down in the only armchair. Soon he got quite absorbed in the cartoon. He was almost regretful when it finished and the RAI announcer came on with a news-flash.

'We repeat the news that the treasurer of the Rome Christian Democrats and manager of the Banco Nazionale Piemontese, Arrigo Furlani, was this morning kidnapped in Via . . .'

'That's better,' said Arrigo Furlani.

'The chauffeur of the kidnapped man was brutally murdered, and in the subsequent police action three members of the gang were killed.'

'*Povero Aldo*,' breathed Mario. '*Povero*—'

'Shut up! I'm listening,' snapped Furlani.

'According to police sources, Furlani was driven away in a car containing three other members of the Red League.'

'Ha! I should be so lucky!' said Mario in disgust.

The announcer disappeared, and the screen was taken over by the scene of carnage in Via Sparafucile. In the portals of the Bank the underlings, who had remained so conspicuously inconspicuous during the attack, emerged wringing their hands to be interviewed for the nation.

'Renato Capucci, under-manager,' said the interviewer.

'You're fired!' snapped Furlani.

'What kind of man is Arrigo Furlani?'

'A great man,' said the under-manager, smiling oilily, as if he knew his boss was watching. 'Great financier, great democrat, warm, lovable, *un gentil uomo*.'

'Ah,' said Arrigo Furlani. 'Better. Go on.'

'Loved by us all. All of us here at the bank knew that in him we had a true father.'

'*Bene!*' said Furlani. '*Un bravo ragazzo!*' Then he was struck by a thought. 'What did he mean, *had*?'

After a while, they ate. Mario cooked some spaghetti on the little oil stove, and heated up a tin with meat sauce in it. He slapped the results down on to two plates, and took one over to Furlani.'

'Eat, pig,' he said jauntily.

'How?' asked Furlani.

So Mario had to sit there, spooning it into his mouth. When they had done, Furlani demanded to go to the lavatory. Mario untied him, poked the gun in his back, and took him to the improvised closet. Furlani blenched at the smell, but bravely went in, slamming the door behind him. He emerged five minutes later.

'My God, what a dump!' he complained. 'Disgusting. You haven't got the first idea of how to treat a hostage.'

They went back to the big room on the first floor. Mario tied up the banker, and then sat down to eat his spaghetti. It was stone cold.

'You'd better untie me next time, and I'll eat my own,' said Furlani spitefully.

'Oh yes? Then I have to keep my gun on you, and mine still gets cold.'

'What kind of Italian is this, who can't eat his spaghetti

with one hand?' demanded Furlani, casting his eyes up to heaven.

By eight o'clock it was time for the Telegiornale. By now the news people had got into their stride over the kidnapping. When the body-strewn street had been covered, and the policemen interviewed (by now there were four kidnappers in the getaway car, spraying bullets in their wake), they portentously announced an appeal from the wife of the kidnapped man.

'Ha! Mariella! Where is she? . . . Ha! Isn't that typical? Look at that hair—she always has that bit dropping over her forehead . . . Sloven!'

Mariella Furlani began her piece, reading it at first as if it were a school exercise.

'Hey!' said Furlani. 'Anyone would think she was reciting Dante!'

Then, caught up like any true Italian by the drama of it, she left her script: there came into her voice that throb of true emotion, that catch that betrays agony, and then by the end there were tears in her eyes and her hands were cupped at the tormentors of her husband in an agony of supplication.

'Better, Mariella. Make them think you care. Don't tell them you're already planning your wardrobe for the funeral . . . *Bambini?* What the hell are you talking about, woman? *Bambini!* The youngest is seventeen and sleeping with a garage owner . . . Oh, very nice, Mariella . . . Emotion . . . *Molto patetico . . . Brava la vedova!*'

Mariella Furlani finished her pathetic plea on an impassioned note. As she came to an end, the camera backed away from her, and Mariella smirked with enormous self-satisfaction and turned her soft brown eyes towards the newsreader.

'Look! See that? The cow! She's making eyes at other men already! She always used to drool over that announcer. I'll show her. Come on! We'll write the ransom note now!'

'I can write the ransom note,' muttered Mario.

'Of course you'll write the ransom note, cretin,' snapped Furlani. 'How would it look if I wrote it myself? What do you usually write it on?'

'Usually? We never done it before. This is our first.'

'Oh, very nice. You choose me to practise on. Aren't I a lucky guy! What did they use with Moro? Brown paper and thick red pen. Come on, write something. Head it *Lega Rossa* . . . *Rossa* with two s's, you idiot. Do you want them to think you're a gang of illiterates?'

Mario wrote with difficulty, but in a half an hour or so the note was ready. It was a demand for one hundred and fifty million lire, penned in thick, uncertain capitals, and it ended with the injunction: GET IT READY. INSTRUCTIONS FOLLOWING. OTHERWISE FURLANI IS A DEAD MAN.

Furlani said: 'Very good. That will terrify them. Supposing they care. Where are you going to post it?'

That had all been taken care of. 'I post this one in Rome. Next one I post in Naples. After that, Pescara.'

'Brilliant. Staggeringly clever. So the carabinieri draw a triangle, and they say where is the middle of that triangle, and we get police swarming up and down the autostrada and looking for deserted castles and palazzi. Bravo Mario! Bravo *Lega Rossa*! Listen to me: you post the first in Rome, the next in Firenze, the next in Torino.'

It was while Mario was away in Rome next day that Arrigo Furlani wriggled himself free of the not very competently tied ropes. When Mario returned from his trip he found him sitting in the one armchair and hungrily forking a plateful of something into his mouth.

'Hey, Mario! Have a good day? You try the cannelloni. It's better than the Bolognese.'

Mario waved the gun uncertainly at him, but soon he got down to heating up a tin, and later when they settled down to the Telegiornale he forgot the gun altogether.

The result of the ransom note was less impressive than

they had hoped. The Banco Nazionale Piemontese, in the person of its national head, appeared on television the next night. The Banco Nazionale if'ed and ah'ed and but'ed: it doubted the wisdom, even while it greatly regretted, and it hoped that these dangerous and conscienceless men . . . Furlani sat before the screen, screaming his outrage at the lack of enthusiasm in their response.

'See? *Ingrati!* Pigs! I work myself into an early heart attack, and see what the response is! I'll cook your goose, Contini,' he yelled at the mournfully regretful and hand-wringing National Chairman of the Banco Piemontese. He felt in the inside pocket of his now very crumpled suit. 'See!' He brandished a piece of paper at the screen. 'I drop my briefcase but I still have *this!* Mario! Quick! Another ransom note!'

And so another note was penned, with less concern about the spelling as they raged over the ingratitude of big capital-ists and their lackeys. In this second note the sum was upped to two hundred million, and Mario added the words: SHALL THE WORLD BE TOLD THE TRUTH ABOUT THE MARCHESE CONTRACT? Furlani smiled bitterly when Mario proudly displayed the completed note.

'Next time we say the Tartini contract. The time after we say the Donatelli contract. And we up the ransom. I've got plenty of truths about plenty of contracts, if that's the way Contini wants to play it.'

That, however, proved unnecessary. Mario drove to Firenze the next day. ('Pick up some fresh meat, for God's sake, and some vegetables. You're ruining my digestion with these tins. And pick up a reasonable Chianti—nothing special or someone will wonder, with your appearance.') By the following evening the Bank was grovelling all over the news media in its eagerness to fulfil the conditions of the *Lega Rossa*. The money, the Chairman assured a world less than breathless and mainly interested in whether it could afford its next dish of pasta, was all ready, packed up in used notes, and they waited now only for the instructions concerning the transfer.

Mario had thought about that before. Or rather Aldo and Gianni and the brighter members of the *Lega Rossa* had. Furlani examined the plans as retailed to him (admittedly imperfectly) by Mario, and found them not merely wanting, but positively cretinous.

'Ha! So they wanted to spend the rest of their lives in jail, your idealistic friends, did they? Or was it the courtroom they were really looking forward to? "Prisoners at the bar, have you anything to say?"—and they spout twenty-four pages of jargon-ridden garbage and think they've won a glorious victory. Pah! What lunatics! You're well rid of them. Remember—they would have taken you with them. And you wouldn't even have understood the jargon. It's a good job you have me now to look after your interests.'

When he got down to thinking about it and discussing it with Mario, who at least could be used as a sounding-board, the problem sorted itself out into two component parts. One was the actual getting of the money, the second was where to go with it afterwards. The first was the simpler of the two.

'All we have to do is set a place where they are to put the suitcases with the money. A wide open place. If there is a stationary car within miles, we drive on and start again. If this is done, we promise I will be found twelve hours later. We'll go in the car. No—we'll hire a faster one. I'll be bound and handcuffed in the front seat. We'll put a bolster in the back, to represent one of the other men they think we've got, crouched down. Simple. No problem. They won't dare to try anything, in case they have a corpse on their hands. The problem is, where we go afterwards.'

'Where we go afterwards,' said Mario obediently.

'There's North Africa. We could hire a boat. You could. False passports. Probably slip in unobserved, with those dumbchucks down there . . . Still, all those damned Arabs. I've never really fancied North Africa. Probably have some fanatic take over and turn it into a strict Islamic state.'

He thought about the penalty for theft in Islam, and looked down apprehensively at his hands.

'What about Switzerland, then? Very picturesque. Good, good place for bankers.'

But when he thought about it, he didn't greatly fancy Switzerland either. All those mountains—so fatiguing for a man of his build. And cows. And lymphatic women. And the lousy weather and the lack of coastline.

When he thought about it, the only country he really fancied was Italy. And in this Mario agreed. They got quite sentimental about it.

'With all its faults,' announced Furlani expansively, 'with all this damned terrorism, all this corruption, the Mafia, all the rest, it's still the best country in the world for a civilized man, for a man of enterprise.'

'*È vero!*' shouted Mario. '*Viva l'Italia!*'

They drank a couple of glasses of Chianti to it, and got very cosy, and it was in this mood of sentimental nationalism that Arrigo Furlani got his idea.

'I have it! Ha-ha! Literally I have it! I have a little estate —a *proprietà*—'

'But that's impossible!' protested Mario.

'Not in my own name, you understand. Secret. Totally secret. For purposes of—what shall we call it?—tax adjustment. I own it in the name of Luciano Doretti. I have been there—what?—three times. With a young lady. With three young ladies. Hardly a soul has seen us. I have dark glasses on, a little false beard. Now—see!—I have a real beard.' He fingered the thick stubble. 'The perfect plan!'

'Where is this estate?' asked Mario.

'Between Firenze and Siena, but way off the motorway. Perfect! Lonely. But good neighbours too. Good class. Tuscan aristocrats, English intellectuals. After a year or two we could mix. I could mix. Is perfect!'

And that was how they did it. Six days later, in a very

fast hired car, with smoked glass windows, they retrieved two suitcases full of notes (they checked that before they drove off) from a lonely stretch of road deep in the Mezzogiorno. Mario drove with a new confidence, and when they were well away he even began to sing—love songs, happy songs, songs sung rather better by Caterina Valente. Furlani did not stop him. He was feeling almost benevolent.

He had insisted on going to the assignation bound and gagged, which showed a commendable sense of verisimilitude, as well as a sensible desire to save his own skin. He had insisted on Mario keeping a gun in his hand during the actual retrieval of the money. After all, the plan might have misfired. But nothing went wrong. They drove and drove in the summer sun, up the eastern coast of Italy. Sometimes they stopped for a drink—and poured liberal glasses of real French brandy, and laughed and horsed around. Then Furlani demanded to be bound and gagged again, and they continued on their way. Often they listened to the car radio: Radio Italy was reporting that the Banco Nazionale Piemontese was cautiously optimistic that its revered manager would be free in a few hours' time, certain measures having been taken. Mario threw back his head and roared, and Furlani sniggered through his gag.

It was a time of suspense for a lot of people. The Chairman of the Banco Nazionale sat in his head office, hoping that at last (one way or another) the lid had been shut down tight on the question of the Marchese contract. And in her substantial bourgeois home in the centre of Rome, surrounded by yapping dogs and two consoling maids, Mariella Furlani sat on the sofa, picking with long painted fingernails at a tiny handkerchief, letting out little whimpers of anguish, and hoping against hope. Surely it was possible, even at this stage, that something would still go wrong?

Long after nightfall, Furlani and Mario arrived at his estate of Campo-Castella, five miles from the tiny village of Bandolero. Everything was in total darkness.

'Untie me,' hissed Furlani. Unhesitatingly Mario obeyed.

'Put the car in the garage,' whispered Furlani. 'Tomorrow we'll abandon it somewhere. Torino, perhaps. I have the house-key on my keyring.'

He opened the front door of the farm house, and cautiously put on the light. Presently Mario came in with the suitcases.

'Nice,' he said. 'Is very nice.'

'We'll make it better,' said Furlani. 'Can you paper? It needs to be lived in. And we'll buy another car. A Mercedes.'

'Ai! Mercedes!' howled Mario in rapture. He put down the suitcases, and finally threw the gun down on the splendid oak dining table.

'Careful! It's antique!' snapped Furlani. But then a better mood overtook him.

'We're safe!' he shouted.

'Safe!' yelled Mario. And they sang and danced, and then they yelled in triumph and danced a bit more, little jigs of happiness. Then they poured out large glasses of whisky, and Furlani found some ice in the refrigerator. They opened the cases again, and feasted their eyes on the money. Mario took one bundle up, and gazed on it with reverence. Then he split open the wrapping band, and threw the hundred notes from the bundle into the air. They seemed to his child-like gaze to float, there in the musty air—to float in infinite promise. Furlani took up a bundle too, and threw it into the air. Then they pelted each other, and then they grovelled around like babies in the thick carpet of *lire*.

Once in the course of their night-long binge of triumph Furlani did look at the gun on the table. It would be so easy to finish off Mario now, and bury him in the grounds. But Furlani was essentially a man of peace. Corrupt, and a bully, but essentially a man of peace. And really, what would be the point? Mario was a good boy. Almost a son to him. And very stupid. He wouldn't give him any trouble. And after all, he was going to need a chauffeur.

BLOWN UP

'Would you like another cheese and onion twisty?' asked Annie Monkton from the passenger seat, pushing the bag in the direction of the steering-wheel.

'No, thanks, Ma, I'm happy with the prawn cocktail crisps,' said her son Herbie, speeding up the M1, but brandishing the bag with his free hand.

'You like those, don't you? I like them now and *again* . . .'

'Have one, Ma.'

'Ta, I don't mind if I do.'

Her arm wobbled over towards the bag, and her elbow pushed itself companionably into her son's comfortable belly. Herbie was six foot three and 305 pounds, and Annie was five foot six and 200 pounds, so their bodies in the little Fiat were touching constantly. But they'd had many trips over the years in the small car, and had learnt to cope without friction.

'That was nice, for a change,' said Annie, munching. 'Tasty. Do you remember that seafood cocktail we had at the Monk's Head in Kendal that year?'

'How could I forget it?' said Herbie enthusiastically. 'It was brilliant! It had everything: prawn, crab, cod, smoked haddock. It was Dad recommended that hotel.'

'He was good on hotels, was your dad. He could be a miserable bugger, as you well know, but he knew his hotels. It was him having been a traveller, I suppose.'

'Yes, you'd remember, wouldn't you, where you'd had a really good nosh-up, and where it hadn't come up to standard.'

They sped through the county of Nottinghamshire, their eyes on the highway, except when they dropped to the bags in their hands.

'I've got some coconut ice in my handbag,' said Annie. 'Fancy a bit, son?'

'No, I think I'll stick with the smoked almonds.'

They munched contentedly. Herbie was thinking.

'Do you remember that coconut ice we got in the market in Leeds last year—with all the glacé bits in, and the peel?'

'I do. It was scrumptious. I've often thought about that coconut ice.'

'Now,' said Herbie, when he had got his thoughts in order, 'what I'm wondering is, are we going to stop for lunch at the White Hart in Hunstable, or at the Fox and Newt in Carditch? Or we could even try the Mayflower at Kirkby again.'

'Is that the pub your father took us to? Said he'd had a marvellous rump steak there that nearly filled the plate? Then when he took us it was very disappointing. Mingy little portions, and tough at that, and hardly enough chips to feed a baby.'

'It'd changed management.'

'It had. They ought to warn people. I remember your dad after that meal. Hardly said a word all afternoon. No, thank you, we won't try there again. I won't be done twice over. Let's see, the White Hart's where they do that lovely steak and mushroom pie, isn't it?'

'That's right. Massive portions. With jacket potatoes with grated cheese on.'

'Oh yes. I remember that. Melted in the mouth. And the Fox and Newt's where we had that lovely plaice and chips, where the chips was practically unlimited.'

'That's right. I don't know when I've had better plaice and chips.'

'Still, I think I fancy the steak and mushroom today. We'll have time to digest it before we have our dinner.'

So they stopped at the White Hart, and it hadn't changed hands, and they had the steak and mushroom, and the potatoes with the melted cheese, and a very generous helping

of boiled carrots, and Annie washed hers down with a gin
and tonic, and Herbie washed his down with a pint of
bitter. And just when they thought they'd finished, Herbie
wondered whether he couldn't manage a piece of that Black
Forest gâteau he'd seen at the food bar, and Annie wondered
whether she couldn't too, and she said she'd buy another
round of drinks to go with it, if Herbie would just fetch them
from the bar. So they had the gâteau too, and another round
of drinks, and they were very pleased they did.

'That was lovely,' Annie said. 'That was almost as good
as the Black Forest gâteau they serve at the King's Head in
Shoreditch. You know, the one your dad always swore by.'

'That's right. He loved his Black Forest gâteau, didn't
he? We must go out to the King's Head again some time.
We haven't been there since he died.'

'Not since he had his Attack, in actual fact . . . I didn't
like it after your dad had his Attack. I mean, we couldn't
get around like we'd been used to, could we? . . . Still I
must say that gâteau we've just had was almost as good,
and a very nice-sized portion too. That should keep us going
until dinner.'

As they went towards the car, Annie said:

'Even your dad would have been satisfied with that meal.
Walter was always less snappy when he'd really got his
money's worth, wasn't he?'

They opened the boot, and Annie got out her large holdall
and took from it a supersize bar of fruit and nut, some
liquorice comfits, and a bag of bacon munchies. Herbert
took a packet of potato sticks and a tin of cashews, because,
as he said, he'd had enough sweet things for the moment.
They drove on, out of Nottinghamshire and into Yorkshire,
perfectly happy.

'I like Yorkshire,' said Annie. 'They always do you proud
in Yorkshire.'

'They know how to appreciate food in the North,' said
Herbie.

'They do. You can see it in the people.'

'The question is,' said Herbie, lighting up a cigarette between the potato sticks and the cashews, 'are we going to drive on up to the Lake District tonight, or are we going to stop off in Yorkshire somewhere?'

'Oh, I thought we'd agreed. Stop off. No point in overdoing it. We're not in a race. We've got the whole weekend, and we don't have to be home till Monday night. There's lots of lovely hotels in Yorkshire where they always make you ever so welcome. There's Manor Court, just outside Ilkley, where they do that marvellous table d'hôte for six pounds fifty a head . . .'

They talked over the various alternatives, and finally decided to save Manor Court for the Sunday on the way back, and to spend the night at the Devonshire Arms in Spenlow. They enjoyed a pre-dinner lager and lime in the bar while they went through the menu. Finally Herbie ordered the smoked salmon, followed by sirloin steak with French fries, while Annie ordered the seafood platter, followed by fillet of pork Wellington. Herbie had a pint of bitter at table, and Annie a snowball, and they were as near as possible in a state of perfect bliss until Annie, over the pork Wellington, which as she happily observed nearly covered the plate, suddenly remembered something.

'Here,' she said, 'it's just come to me. The Devonshire Arms was the last place we ever stayed at with your dad. Last trip we ever had. We stayed here at the Devonshire Arms on the way down from Skye and the Western Isles.'

'Did we, Ma? I'd never have remembered that.'

'Well, you should. Three days later he had his first Attack.'

'I remember it was soon after we'd got back from somewhere.'

'And do you know what he had for his dinner that night? Fillet of pork Wellington!'

For a moment the remembrance of things past seemed to cast a shadow over the meal. Annie looked at the great expanse of pork that had been set before her, and she gave the dead Walter the tribute of a passing sigh. Then she took a sup of her snowball, smiled at her son, and set to with a will again.

'Doesn't do to take things like that, does it?' she said.

'Thinking won't bring him back,' said Herbie.

So they didn't think about him.

Next morning they had an English breakfast of egg, bacon, sausage, tomatoes, mushrooms and fried potatoes, with the Yorkshire addition of black pudding, which Herbie pronounced 'not bad, but I don't think I'd want it as a regular thing.' He considered the porridge excellent, though, especially with the golden syrup over, and Annie gave her blessing to the marmalade.

'It's my big criteria,' she said, 'to tell a good hotel from a second-rater. That's none of your cheap stuff—' and she waved her pudgy hand at the pot—'because there's no question of skimping here.'

When they'd paid their bill, Herbie humped their luggage to the car—just the one small case, because Herbie hated lugging heavy cases, and considered it shortened your life span—and they set off again.

'People are silly, giving up good English breakfasts,' said Annie as they drove out of the hotel drive. 'They set you up for the day.'

She slipped into her mouth a piece of chocolate nougat and chewed contentedly.

'That meal last night,' she said, 'the pork Wellington, would have been one of the last good meals your dad ever ate. Apart from the ones I cooked him, of course. The *very* last meal he ate out. He liked eating out, your dad. I never knew a better judge of whether he'd had value for money.'

'Wasn't any point in him eating out, not after his Attack,' said Herbie. 'Not with the sort of stuff he was allowed to eat.'

'No. Imagine going into an Italian restaurant and saying

"I want a nice piece of boiled fish, and some boiled potatoes to go with it." They'd have split their sides laughing.'

'I don't think Dad had the *heart* to eat out again,' said Herbie.

'That's it. It was funny, really. Do you remember that mini-cruise we took to Norway—ooh, back in '70 or '71 it must have been—and how Dad hated all that boiled fish and boiled potatoes we had? It was boiled potatoes with every meal, wasn't it? Just the most uninteresting way of having potatoes, *I* always say. Your dad was really disgusted, considering the price we'd paid. And then when he comes out of hospital, to have to have boiled fish and boiled potatoes and all that horrible invalid food. It was almost as if the doctor who drew up the diet sheet knew about Dad's likes and dislikes, and was trying to get his own back . . . Because your dad was not an easy patient . . . Short-tempered . . .'

'Well, you was very good to him, Ma. You cooked it all for him, didn't you?'

'I did, though it turned my stomach sometimes, quite apart from the extra work. I mean, the only thing we could've eaten that was on his diet was the shepherd's pie, and he wasn't to have that more than once a week. So there was his little messes to do, on top of the things for ourselves . . . It was pitiful watching him eating it . . .'

'And watching *him* watching *us*, eh, Ma?'

Annie Monkton gurgled a little laugh.

'Well, he *was* a picture, I'll give you that. But I still think it was diabolical, that diet sheet. It can't have been necessary. I'm no doctor, but I do know a grown man's got to eat enough to keep body and soul together. To see him sitting there with his pea soup, and the rusk he ·vas suppose to have with it, while we were tucking in to the steak pizzaiola with the sauté potatoes and the baked aubergines —well, I said at the time it wasn't right.'

'I think it was the sweets that got him most, Ma. That

Peach Melba you used to make, with the thick whipped cream and the black cherry jam on top. He used to look at that, gaze you might say, like he was transfixed, like he begrudged us every mouthful . . . We haven't had your Peach Melba lately, have we, Ma?'

'Here, don't go so fast,' said Annie, as they sped along the shores of Lake Windermere. 'We don't want to get to Keswick too early for lunch.'

They both had fresh salmon for lunch, with French fries, peas and beans. 'You pay for Scottish salmon,' said Herbie, 'but it does have that touch of class.' The thought of how much they'd paid for the salmon made them shake their heads reluctantly over the cheese and walnut gâteau. Afterwards they both had a little nap in the car park of the Keswick hotel where they'd eaten, and then Herbie got out his map and they decided where to stay for the night, nibbling at a little bag of savoury sticks. It was a question of whether to go over to Buttermere and then on to the coast and stay at Whitehaven, or whether to take a leisurely trip around Ullswater and overnight at Penrith.

'I'd go for Penrith,' said Annie. 'The Borderer at Penrith. I've got a fancy to try their venison again. I know it's extravagant, but we *are* on holiday.'

Annie had woken from her nap with her mind greatly refreshed.

'Do you know,' she said as they started, 'I don't think they put as much fruit in fruit and nut chocolate as they used to. Or as much nut, come to that.'

'That's the way the cookie crumbles,' said Herbie, not altogether appositely.

They drove along the north shores of Ullswater, passing as they did so, though without seeing them, several hosts of golden daffodils.

'This is a good road now,' said Herbie, increasing the speed. 'A sight better than when we first came up, eh, Ma? Then you really had to dawdle round, because of the potholes.'

But his mother's mind was on other things.

'I didn't *really* enjoy your father's gazing at us eating, like he used to after his Attack,' she said, switching from the fruit and nut to the peppermint fondant. 'I'm not cruel, you know that, Herbie. In fact, though it was a bit of a laugh at first, after a time I found it really put me off my food. Being watched like that. I just wasn't enjoying it any more. I remember sitting there eating a slice of one of my homemade pork pies —with all that lovely jelly, just as I like it—and your dad was toying with his omelette and looking at my plate greedily (because, not to speak ill of the dead, he could be greedy, your dad), and I thought: I can't enjoy this like I should be doing, not with him looking on like he wanted to grab every forkful from me. It was as much as I could do to finish it.'

'Perhaps he should have ate separately, Ma.'

'That would have been like putting him into an insulation ward. No, no, we was a family, and we ate as a family . . . I must say I was glad when they said he could start relaxing the diet.'

Herbie shifted into lower gear up a hill, and dipped into his bag of salt and vinegar flavoured crisps.

'I think they meant gradually, Ma.'

'Well, of course! That was how we went, wasn't it? The whole of the first week we hardly changed his old diet at all. I just gave him a bit of stewed apple or a tiny bit of jam roly-poly for afters. I said to him, I said: "Keep well *under* for the first few days, then you can go *over* on Sunday, have a bit of a blow-out."'

Herbie was quiet for a bit, then he said:

'Well, he enjoyed it, I will say that.'

'Oh, he did. He'd been looking forward to it all week. You could feel the juices running. We talked it all over, you know. There was the lobster pâté, which was his favourite as starters, with the little fingers of buttered toast. Then there was the pork steaks with the mushroom cream sauce that he loved, and the scalloped potatoes and the glazed carrots and the cauliflower in cheese sauce. Then there was the Madeira chocolate cake with the sherry cream topping —the one I got the recipe for out of *Woman's Own*. We'd planned it all. It was a lovely meal.'

'A meal fit for a king,' admitted Herbie.

'And I didn't make any trouble over cooking it, though none of it was convenience foods. I had to do it all with my own hands, but it was a pleasure to me to do it. I loved cooking it for him.'

'And he loved eating it,' said Herbie. 'Even the chocolate cake.'

'Well, it was the best I'd ever made. I thought so myself when I ate up the rest the next day. It was perfection. Maybe it was *so* good that in a way he . . . couldn't stand it.'

'It wasn't a bad way to go,' said Herbie.

'It was a very *good* way to go. I hope I go like that when my time comes. And it was quick too. We'd hardly got him upstairs into the bed before he was gone. A darned sight better than lingering, that's what *I* say.'

'It's what I'd call a good death.'

'So would I. And I'd have been almost happy about it, if it hadn't been for that bleeding doctor,' said Annie, getting almost agitated, and taking out of her handbag a tiny handkerchief, which she dabbed at her eyes.

'Dr Causeley?' said Herbert, surprised. 'He never said anything out of turn in the bedroom.'

'No. It was when he came downstairs. I never told you this, son, because I thought it would make you wild. I'd gone downstairs, being upset, to have a bit of a weep by the fire in the dining-room. And he came downstairs and he came in, and he was just starting to say something when— well, you see, the plates with the sweets was still on the table, with his bit of chocolate cake still unfinished, which had gone to my heart when I came in, and he saw that, and he saw the other plates which was piled on the sideboard, and he looked at them—in*spect*ed I'd call it, in a thoroughly nasty way that he'd no call to adopt—and he said had he been eating this? and I said yes, and explained we'd been sort of saving up on the calories, so he could have one good blow-out. And he said, "What exactly did he have?" and so I told him. And do you know what he said?'

'No, Ma. What did he say?'

'He said: "That meal killed him as surely as if you'd laced it with strychnine."'

Herbie didn't go wild, but he thought for a bit.

'That wasn't very nice of him.'

'It was diabolical. You could have knocked me down with a feather! Me just widowed not five minutes since.'

'It was a liberty. These professional people take too much on themselves.'

'They do. Your dad always said that. It was a wicked, cruel thing to say. And you notice he never had any doubt about signing the death certificate ... That's why I changed my doctor ... I never could fancy going back to Dr Causeley after that ... I know I haven't got anything to reproach myself with ...'

They went quiet for a bit, and Annie Monkton found a sucky sweet in her bag and comforted herself with that. Quite soon they were drawing up in the courtyard of the Borderer. Herbie got out, and made sure they'd got rooms. Luckily the tourist season was only just beginning. He came back smiling.

'Couldn't be better. Two nice singles. I took a peek at the dinner menu, Ma. You'll be able to have the venison. I've worked up an appetite, so I think I'm going to fancy the mixed grill.'

As he took the case from the boot and they started towards the main door, Annie's good humour returned. She nudged Herbie with her fat arm.

'It's nice being on our own, though, isn't it, son?'

A PROCESS OF REHABILITATION

'I don't know I'm sure,' said Bessie Hargreaves, shaking her head. It was a white head, but the gentle curls suggested that she was a woman who would never willingly let herself go. 'I've never heard of such a thing.'

'Oh, it's a very well-established scheme,' said young Mr Bateson from the Probation Office brightly. He meant to reassure her, but he only filled her with the realization that she was very out of touch with contemporary life. 'It's part of the process of rehabilitation. They're only minor offenders, and they're put to work of local usefulness instead of sending them to jail. You see, what they learn in jail can often turn them into criminals for life, whereas with this scheme they're doing something constructive—it's almost like learning a trade.'

'I suppose that's true,' admitted Mrs Hargreaves.

'This lad I was thinking of sending along to help you with the redecoration: he's just a young football hooligan—'

'I wouldn't want anyone violent,' Bessie Hargreaves said quickly.

'Oh, he's nothing worse than destructive. With all this youth unemployment around, it's sometimes the only way they can express themselves. It's their way of getting through to society—you can almost see it as *con*structive, in a sense. And he's quite a handy lad. The house could do with a bit of maintenance and a lick of paint,' he added, looking around in his casually insulting way, 'as I'm sure you'd agree.'

'I've done what I could,' said Bessie Hargreaves defensively. Then she admitted: 'It has been let go a bit.'

'It could be made very nice.'

'We'd only been married five years when my husband

died, you see. It's been a struggle to keep it on, even though it's only a terrace house. I could never afford to have the work done . . .'

'We'd share the cost of the materials,' said the young man, 'and of course the labour would be free. It would work out very well for you. Now, what do you say?'

Bessie Hargreaves sat looking at her hands, shaking her head almost imperceptibly. Finally she said: 'I suppose it'd be what you might call a good deed.'

'It would. It would indeed.'

She took a deep breath.

'All right. You can send him along.'

Bessie Hargreaves quite enjoyed going round to the Do It Yourself centre that was ten minutes away, and choosing paint and a bit of wallpaper for her own bedroom. She kept telling herself it was as long as she could remember since anything had been done to the house. But all the time there was, niggling at the back of her mind, this worry about the young man who was coming. What would he be like? And she told herself that it was the situation that worried her. Something new, something . . . almost, it seemed, threatening. Already she found that in her mind she was calling him 'the thug'. She would be glad when it was over.

She was sweeping the kitchen floor on Wednesday morning when he arrived, not more than ten minutes after the appointed time. He was a strong, thickset young man of about twenty, uncouth yet perhaps not ill-intentioned. He walked in his heavy shoes over her newly-swept floor, but then said 'Sorry' and took them off in the hall. She swept up the little scraps of mud, then went into the hall, almost shyly.

'Where do we start, then?' asked the young man.

'I thought in the living-room,' said Bessie Hargreaves. 'It's where I mostly am, and it *would* be brighter for a coat of paint.'

'Right you are,' said the boy, and followed her into the

room, where she had already laid a covering of newspapers over the floor. He looked around. 'No problem here, not if we just tidy up the wallpaper and paint over it.'

'I thought that's what we should do,' said Bessie, nodding, 'seeing as you've just got the week. You see, I didn't know about wallpapering, but I did buy a bit of bright, flowery paper for my bedroom. It was *such* a cheerful pattern . . .'

'I can try,' said the boy. 'I helped me mam with a bit of papering, just before she took off. It won't be professional, but I'll do the best I can.'

'That will be nice. Would you like a cup of tea—er, I'm not sure I caught your name.'

'Brian. Me mates call me Bri.'

Mrs Hargreaves didn't feel quite up to Bri, so she said: 'Do you take sugar, Brian?'

While they had their tea they got almost friendly, with Brian coming down off his ladder, where he'd been preparing the ceiling, and sipping his sweet, hot brew over by the fireplace.

'Did your mother leave you, did you say?' asked Mrs Hargreaves, with a shocked expression on her face.

'That's right. Took off wi' a fancy man. Never seen her in me life sin'.'

'What happened to you, then?'

'They put me in an institution. It weren't that bad. Then me auntie took me on.'

'Do you still live with her?'

'Yeah. We get on all right. She gets a bit pissed off, what wi' me being around all day, but there's nowt to be done about that. We don't fight that much.'

Mrs Hargreaves was going to say more, perhaps about how grateful he must be to his aunt, but then—was it fancy, or was he really eyeing her lovely silver frame, the one she'd picked up in that junk shop all those years ago for half-a-crown, with that picture of her and Walter at Scarborough in it? No—probably it was her imagination.

On the other hand . . . what did he mean when he said he and his aunt didn't *fight* that much? The boy—young man, really—drank down his tea and bounded up the ladder again, and as he stood there, so high, so masterfully above her, she could not help noticing how broad his shoulders were, and how thick his arms, and when she felt that impression of youth and power a sharp dagger of fear stabbed her. She wouldn't have a chance . . .

Still, they got on all right that day. Brian's interest in that silver frame seemed perfectly natural when, later on, darting down from his ladder to refill his paint tray with matt white for the ceiling, he said casually:

'That you and your old man?'

'That's right. When we were young.' Bessie added sadly: 'He was never anything else. We only had the five years.'

The boy seemed almost touched. Anyway he didn't ask any more questions, but hopped up his ladder and got on with his job. When he had to go out to his little cart of tools and equipment that he'd left by the gate, he always put on and took off his shoes by the back door.

'I can see you like to keep the place tidy,' he said.

'Well, I *do*,' Bessie agreed. 'I've always liked to keep things spick and span, even when I've not had much to *keep* clean. But you can't expect not to get a bit of dirt in when you're decorating.'

The living-room took a good two days' work, and when it was finished Bessie decided the boy had done a good, if rough, job of work. There were places one shouldn't look at too closely, but the general effect was greatly improved. It was really bright, almost cheerful.

The boy himself—well, he didn't improve on acquaintance. And yet, it wasn't quite that. It was just that, as he felt more at home in the house, and with her, he got more relaxed, and more . . . more familiar, unbuttoned, more what she took to be his real brash self. Was he just brash—

what Bessie called to herself 'lippy'? Or was there something more? Something almost . . . brutal?

On the second evening, when Bessie was pottering around cleaning up newspapers from the floor, Brian went over without so much as a by-your-leave and picked up the other snapshot in the room, from the window-ledge where it was kept.

'Saw this when I was painting,' he said. 'Is this your son?'

The face in the photograph was that of a young man, not good-looking but cheerful and sunny-faced, taken in the little scrap of garden in the front, in open-necked shirt and flannels.

'Oh no,' Bessie said, her face screwed into a troubled expression. 'We never had no children, Walter and me. We *would* have had, but we never knew there'd be no time. Walter was killed in a pit accident, you see.'

'Who's this, then?'

'That was Tom Taylor. He lodged here for a bit. He was an apprentice at Sawley's—you know, the cotton mill.'

'Looks a jolly chap.'

'Oh, he was. Always cheery.'

'Do you keep in touch?'

'Oh no, no. It wasn't to be expected.'

'You ought to have. You need some young chap like that to look after you.'

He'd like to move in, Bessie said to herself. He'd like to move in here with me and live off me. I bet his aunt takes most of his dole money, and he thinks I'd be a softer touch.

'Oh, I can take care of myself, never you mind,' she said. 'I've had to.'

Before he embarked on the bedroom he painted all the doors in the house a glossy white. He wanted time to think about the papering, remembering how it should be done. The weather had turned hot, and he just wore a T-shirt and jeans under his overalls. There was nothing personal of Mrs Hargreaves's in the hall or the landing, so when they had tea or coffee, or when he ate the 'snap' that he brought with him for his lunch, he started talking about himself. If he did want Mrs Hargreaves to take him in, he certainly chose the wrong subjects.

'Got in a fight down at t'pub last night,' he would say. 'Supped too much black 'n' tan. So had t'other bugger, come to that. Must've bin barmy, me still being on probation. Still, landlord didn't call the police. He just showed us the door, so there was no harm done.'

'What were you quarrelling about?' Mrs Hargreaves asked, envisaging a girl, or politics, or some bet or other.

'Can't rightly remember,' said Brian, scratching his head and grinning ruefully.

Her fear suddenly shot into her mind a picture of this boy, this young thug, breaking her as a child breaks a cheap toy—no, as the cook in the café she had once worked in had quartered a chicken, the brittle bones snapping under her capable knife. She nearly panicked, but she controlled herself enough to collect up the cups.

'I don't approve of all this violence,' she said.

'Not likely you would,' said Brian equably. 'I think it were a bit daft meself.'

But his life of dole and emptiness didn't have many highlights, and getting into 'a bit of a scrap' was among those few. So that, when he talked to her, it was quite often of that, or scrapes he'd been in at school or the orphanage, or riots at the local football ground at the end of matches.

'I got in there and I put me boot into one of the Everton supporters,' he would say, 'then I smashed me fist into the face of another, and I got a third before the police picked me up. It was great!'

Sometimes after these conversations Bessie Hargreaves felt quite sick. It was the sickness of fear.

After the weekend Brian got down to the bedroom. He had had to report to the local police at the time of the local soccer team's match, so he had no violent encounters to narrate. Before he came on Monday Bessie had removed her little tin box of jewellery from the bedroom, and hidden it in the kitchen cabinet. There was nothing of any great value in it, but most of it had been given her by Walter, and there was the little Christmas brooch from her lodger Tom Taylor that she set an oddly high price on. And apart from the pieces with sentimental value, there *was* that amethyst bracelet that had been Walter's mother's that she was always meaning to take and have valued. So she took the box and hid it away from 'the young thug's' prying gaze.

Brian, when he came, was not interested in any personal mementoes in the bedroom; he was more taken up by the techniques of wallpapering. Some things he remembered, some he had talked over with his mates during the weekend. He had most of the right ideas, and the problems, when they came up, he solved by an innate practicality. During the morning he discussed them as they arose with Bessie, and this kept him off dangerous subjects. After lunch, as he prepared for the afternoon's work, he talked with the amused condescension of the young about his auntie, and from her he got on to the subject of his mother.

'It's my belief—thinking it over, like—that she took off because she knew she wouldn't be able to cope wi' me much longer. I were twelve, but I were big. She'd managed up to then, but she knew she couldn't much longer.'

'You must have been a right handful, if your own mother couldn't manage you,' said Bessie timorously.

'Aye, I were. Mind you, she'd a quick hand, and she could really sting if she got one in when I weren't looking. But you get used to that, don't you? Mind you, I bet her fancy man gave her a worse time than I ever would've, so that must've served the old duck right.'

'You shouldn't speak of your mother like that,' said Bessie.

'What did she ever do for me?' Brian asked, reasonably.

Bessie was appalled by the new view Brian gave her of

family relationships—loveless, antagonistic, cruel. It would never have been like that if she had had a child. What could you expect of a boy who had grown up in that sort of atmosphere? She looked at Brian standing there, a spatula in his powerful right hand, and she looked down in fear, excused herself, and went downstairs.

He really got on fast that day, and since he would finish on the Tuesday, Bessie thought she ought to make some gesture of appreciation. Just before the shops shut she pottered down to the butcher's and got some pork. She'd make one of her pork pies—she hadn't made one in years, not since Tom Taylor was lodging with her. She baked it that evening. The pastry was difficult, because the let-down flap on her kitchen cabinet, on which she kneaded and rolled it, had become very rickety. But even so, when she took it out of the oven it looked a picture, and smelt a dream.

Her bedroom, next day, looked a picture too. Brian had only one wall to do, a long, flat, uncomplicated wall. Bessie had bought a pretty strip of border to put round the room under the picture rail. When everything was done, they stood surveying it together—light, flowery, really pretty.

'I reckon I could do this for a living,' said Brian.

'I reckon you could,' said Mrs Hargreaves. 'You've done a right good job . . . I've baked something for you.'

'Baked something?'

'Yes—well, for us. A little thank-you. I thought you deserved one, after all the work you've put in. My pork pies used to be famous.'

'I like a nice bit o' pork pie,' said Brian.

They sat on the bed eating, and they looked around the room commenting admiringly on what a difference the new wallpaper made. Brian said he had never tasted pork pie like it, and it really knocked the shop jobs into a cocked hat, didn't it?

'It *is* very nice,' said Bessie, trying not to boast. She'd have felt pretty insulted if he hadn't thought it better than the shop jobs. 'It's not quite my best. I haven't made hot-water pastry in years, and the flap on my kitchen cabinet is so rocky that I couldn't really go at the kneading properly.'

'I've got the afternoon,' said Brian. 'I'll see if I can fix it for you.'

'Oh, there's no call,' said Mrs Hargreaves, becoming agitated yet trying to hide it. 'You've done your jobs, like I agreed with the probation man. And I make so little pastry these days, being on my own.'

'No trouble,' said Brian, getting up. 'I'll get it fixed, and have me other bit o' pie when I'm done. I've got a saw and chisel in me barrow.'

'No, no, really,' Bessie called weakly, but he was down and out to his barrow before she could follow him more slowly down the stairs. By the time she reached the kitchen he was back in there, and taking down the flap of the kitchen cabinet. Bessie stood in the doorway, transfixed by the sight of her little box of trinkets, sitting there on the shelf above the flour and the rice and the cake-mixes.

Brian didn't notice it at all. He had laid a big, threatening saw and a long chisel on the kitchen table, and he was pulling the flap up and down.

'Aye, it's rocky,' he said. 'I think it must be the supports underneath.'

Bessie watched, horrified, as her little box jumped up and down on the shelf, and as if in a dream she moved round the kitchen, skirting those terrifying tools on the table, and stood against the draining-board, on which the breadknife still lay among her breakfast washing-up. Brian picked up the big saw and looked at it.

'I'll not need that,' he said. 'There's nowt wrong wi' the flap. But I'll get at the supports wi' this.'

He picked up the chisel, and stood there considering, stroking it with his hand. At the sight of the big lad with the threatening tools in his hand Bessie's hand had gone behind her and clutched comfortingly to the breadknife.

'I'll just take a bit off one o' them supports,' said Brian, still caressing his chisel. Then he took up the flap again and banged it down to establish the provenance of its ricketiness. The box jumped up and down on its shelf, and finally rolled down over the bags of flour and emptied in pathetic profusion on to the flap its contents of trinkets and jewellery.

'Well—that's a funny thing to keep in your kitchen cupboard,' said Brian, smiling down from his young height at the display, and not seeing as Bessie darted forward and plunged the kitchen knife cleanly into his stomach, over and over, fearfully, fatally, until he rolled over on to the floor, his face creased into an expression of agony and inquiry.

'It was something we never thought about,' said young Mr Bateson at the Probation Office, shaking his head. 'I mean, you check out on the offenders, but you wouldn't think you'd need to check out on the old people they're supposed to help.'

'Incipient paranoia,' said his superior, looking up from the report. 'Of course, she was released from the Institution as cured, two or three years ago. Still, she had killed the lodger. Got the idea that he was going to rape or murder her, and struck him with a knife, just the same way.'

'Whoever would have thought?' said Bateson, shaking his head. 'To me she was just like any other old lady.' He was quiet for a moment, but being a congenitally optimistic young man he shook off his pensiveness and added with a smile: 'Still, there's one good thing, isn't there? The fact that it was that way round means there's no danger to the rehabilitation programme.'

HOLY LIVING AND HOLY DYING

When the act of love was over, or the act of intimacy, or whatever lying euphemism you cared to call it by, Gordon Chitterling rolled over on to his back, stared at the off-brown ceiling, and sighed. The girl, who had said her name was Jackie (didn't they all?) reached over for her cigarettes on the bedside table, took one as if this was an invariable habit, and lit it.

'Come a bit quick, didn't you?' she said, in her horrible Midlands accent. 'You can have another go for an extra twenty. I've nothing fixed till half past eight.'

'I'm not made of money,' said Gordon irritably. 'I'm a journalist.'

'Shouldn't have thought journalists went short,' said Jackie. 'There's a gentleman on the *Sun* has me regular on expenses.'

'That doesn't happen with the *Catholic Weekly*.'

'Is that religious?' Jackie asked, blowing out smoke. Gordon immediately regretted having told her.

'Not really. It means we are catholic in our interests. Wide-ranging,' Gordon lied.

Jackie frowned, trying to understand, but soon gave it up.

'Fifteen,' she said. 'I can't say fairer than that, can I? It'll save me the hassle of going out again.'

Gordon raised his eyebrows to heaven. This was beginning to resemble a street bazaar in Cairo. At any moment she'd be throwing in Green Shield stamps. He jumped off the bed and began pulling on his clothes.

'Some other time,' he said, buttoning his flies. Gordon was one of the few men in London who still had button-up flies. There was an all-or-nothing quality about zips that he distrusted. 'Duty calls,' he added, in his tight-lipped way.

He grabbed at his attaché case, but either because he was clumsy, or because he hadn't shut it properly before, it fell open and spilled its contents on to the linoleumed floor.

'Damn and blast.'

'There, I told you you shouldn't rush away, all excited like that.'

About as worked up as Calvin Coolidge on a wet Monday, thought Gordon, as he bent down to retrieve his papers. Jackie had idly rolled over on the bed to have a look.

'Coo, look at that. It's old Mossy. One of my regulars.'

She was pointing to a large, glossy photograph of a distinguished gentleman in his fifties. Gordon snatched it up.

'You are quite mistaken.'

''Course I'm not. Comes regular. Real old sport. I think he's something in the world of finance.'

'You certainly are mistaken. He was a Bishop.'

'Go on! Well, he never lets on. Dirty old Bish!'

'I mean you are altogether mistaken in the man,' said Gordon, shutting his briefcase with an irritable click. 'You must have confused him with another . . . client. Bishop Bannerman was a highly respected figure in the Catholic Church. In addition to which he is dead.'

'I didn't say he'd been recently.'

'He was a very fine man. Highly respected. Unimpeachable character. Almost saintly.'

He was shutting the door when Jackie shouted:

'And he had a strawberry birthmark the shape of Australia on his left shoulder.'

Gordon gave the game away by his pause after he had shut the door. Jackie must have registered that it was a full ten seconds before he clattered down the bare floorboards on the stairs and out into Wardour Street. In fact, he knew she had registered, because he heard her hideous shrill laugh as he descended.

Gordon Chitterling walked through Soho in the direction of Victoria Street, a frown on his rather insignificant face.

The first thing that concerned him was that Bishop Bannerman might become a subject for scandal and concern—or, rather, that *he* might be the cause of his so becoming. If he hadn't spilled that damned attaché case . . . If he hadn't gone to her straight from work. But somehow it was straight after work that he most felt like it.

His profile of Bishop Bannerman, who had died two months previously, was already fully researched and was only waiting to be written up. The outlines of his career were clear. Born in 1930 into a middle-class family in Warwick, where his father had been a chartered accountant, Anthony Bannerman had begun the process of conversion to Catholicism at the early age of seventeen. Many such early enthusiasms were to be put down to the powerful tug of religion working on the impressionable adolescent mind, but Bannerman's had held, and had stuck with him through university, so that by the time he had his BA, his aim of then studying for the priesthood had been accepted both by the church into which he had been received, and by his family.

After that it had been onwards and upwards: exemplary parish priest, much-loved broadcaster on *Lift Up Your Hearts* and *Thought For The Day*, eventually Bishop of West Ham, and strongly tipped for the Westminster job, when or if it became vacant. That was not to be: he had been struck down by a heart attack while attending a conference in Venice . . . Death in Venice . . . Well, at least he had not been *that* way inclined.

Gordon Chitterling let himself into the *Catholic Weekly* offices, and went along to his own neat little cubicle. There was nobody much about, and he switched on his desk light and sat there thinking. Imagine! that much-loved pastor, that fearless campaigner against apartheid, that helper among AIDS sufferers, that tireless worker for peace and reconciliation in Northern Ireland—to patronize a common prostitute. Regularly. But then, to patronize one regularly would be safer than picking up just anyone off the streets. Safer too to choose an ignorant little tart like Jackie.

Ah well, that was one aspect of the Bishop that would not get into the Profile.

Yet everything else, *everything*, had been so positive, so enthusiastic, so admiring. He opened his bottom drawer, and pulled out the thick sheaf of transcribed interviews. He leafed through them: 'caring pastor' . . . 'concerned, committed crusader' . . . It had all seemed of a piece. Here was the interview with his brother, where he'd talked about the birthmark the shape of Australia: 'He always said it meant he would end up Archbishop of Sydney, but actually he never even went there . . .'

A phrase caught his eye: 'He was essentially a man of the people, among people, at home with people.' He stopped and read on. It was an interview with Father O'Hara, a parish priest in the borough of Camden. It went on:

'I once saw him in a pub in my parish. I'd been visiting the wife of the publican. It was the Duck and Whistle—*not* an up-market pub, in fact rather a dubious place, with a lot of dubious characters among the regulars. Bishop Bannerman was in 'civvies', talking and laughing with Snobby Noakes, a petty crook who'd been in and out of jail. They were completely man-to-man. I even saw money changing hands. I expect he was putting a bet on a horse—something he loved to do now and then. When he saw me he came over, and he talked to me just as naturally as he'd been talking to Snobby. You got the feeling that he'd chat with the Queen in exactly the same way he'd chat with a housewife in a block of council flats. That was the kind of man he was . . .'

It had seemed admirable at the time. The man of God who was at home in all worlds. Now it made Gordon wonder. There was no reason why it should: bishops went into pubs: bishops talked to criminals. The fact that, apparently, on occasion he used a prostitute did not mean there was anything less than innocent about his talking in a pub with a petty criminal.

And yet . . . and yet . . . That money changing hands. Gordon Chitterling did not like that at all.

The next day, when he sat down to write the Profile, his pen seemed to be weighted with lead. Not that his words were normally winged. Gordon was a reliable, competent journalist rather than an inspired one. Yet it was that very reliability that prevented the clichés of his pen-picture attaining any sort of conviction. Words and phrases like 'saintly humility', 'committed campaigner', 'a man of God who was also a man among men' seemed to snicker back at him from the page. 'You don't believe that, do you?' they seemed to say. It is not easy to work for a religious newspaper. You have to believe what you write. So much simpler to work for Murdoch.

To light upon a Bishop who broke his vows worried Gordon. His own sins worried him only a little, but then— he had taken no vows as a reporter on the *Catholic Weekly*. He knew he was going to have to go to the Duck and Whistle. What he was going to do when he got there he did not know, but he knew he was going to have to go.

In the event the Duck and Whistle, over the next two or three weeks, came to know him quite well. It was, as Father O'Hara had said, a decidedly down-market pub, with men doing dubious deals in nooks and corner. There was a juke-box, the blare from which was used to cover muttered conversations. The first evening Gordon spent there Snobby Noakes simply breezed in, downed a whisky and water, and breezed out again. Gordon did no more than identify him, from the landlord's greeting, and the talk of other customers. Snobby was a thin, perky character, rather better or more flashily dressed than the others in the bar. These mostly had a look that was decidedly seedy, and as his visits became regular Gordon—for his was the outlook and talents of the chameleon—came to merge with his surroundings and become seedier: he resurrected an old raincoat, made sure he wore a shirt with frayed cuffs.

His first talk with Snobby was innocuous—about horses and dogs, the kind you bet on, of course. Snobby was man-of-the-world, and rather condescending to Gordon's shabbiness. Snobby had once worked as a bookie's runner, and was adept at the smart disappearance when a big pay-out was due. What Snobby loved, it became apparent in later conversations, was a 'wheeze'—a smart idea for a quick financial killing. Any other kind of killing was way outside his territory, for his heroes were shysters and con men. Where others might hero-worship Cromwell or Napoleon, Snobby saved his admiration for an Horatio Bottomley or a Maundy Gregory.

Gordon he accepted as a small-time con artist, rather on his own level, though less prosperous. 'Though you've got a touch of class in the voice,' he once said, flatteringly. 'You could sell encyclopædias, you could.'

'The best cons,' Snobby would say expansively over a drink, especially if Gordon bought it for him, 'are the simple cons. Look at the South Sea Bubble. Learnt about that at school—always stayed with me. Simple, effective, beautiful!'

Gordon nodded wisely. He was never quite sure when Snobby was being humorous. Snobby had a sense of humour, where Gordon had very little.

'The other thing about your simple con is, it's them that clean up the biggest,' Snobby went on. 'Take the bloke that thought up the wheeze that Venice is sinking. Brilliant. He must have pulled in millions over the years.'

'You're not suggesting Lord Norwich—'

'Whoever he was. Some smart little Mafia con I'd've thought. A real little beauty. Because bleedin' Venice isn't sinking, any more than Southend is. All high and dry and dandy. Mind you the bloke who thought of building it there in the first place was something of an artist too. Did you ever see a more obvious tourist trap? A man ahead of his time he must have been.'

Snobby winked. Quite unprompted by Gordon, the conversation had begun to take a turn he liked.

'You seem taken with Venice,' he said casually.

'Oh, I was. Lovely little place. Only drawback that I could see was you couldn't do a good snatch there, because the getaway presents problems.'

'Been there often?'

'Just the once. A church conference.'

Gordon's heart rose.

'Well!' he said. 'I wouldn't have thought of you as a Christian.'

Snobby laughed.

'That's why I was there, though. The Fourth Ecumenical Conference. You know: Catholic and C. of E. clergymen holding hands in gondolas. *That* was a right occasion. Tell you about it some day.'

He didn't, though, not over the next two evenings spent chewing over the great cons, past and present. In the end Gordon had the brainwave of bringing the conversation round to clergymen.

'I don't know about you,' he said, with the air of long and disreputable experience, 'but I never found there was much to be got out of the clergy. They're supposed to be so bloody other-worldly, but somehow there's never anything much to be got there. Maybe they're too hard up.'

Snobby's face assumed a relishing smile.

'True. Most of them are that. Church of England, anyhow.' He leaned forward confidingly. 'But I'll tell you this, me boy: there's money to be got not *from* the Church, but *by* the Church. That's for sure.'

'What do you mean? Collection boxes, appeals, that kind of thing?' asked Gordon innocently.

'No, I do not mean that at all. Let me put it to you like this: if a man wants to lead a comfortable life, and enjoys tacking over to the windy side of the law, what better trade to enter than the Church? And here I'm talking about the Catholic Church, me boy. Very comfortable life, especially the higher you go. The celibacy rule doesn't bother you, because you've no intention of abiding by it. And as a way into the criminal life it has one great, glorious advantage.'

'What's that?'

'Who hears most secrets? A bank manager? A politician? A social worker? No—it's a priest.'

Gordon's heart almost stopped beating.

'My God—you don't mean—?'

'Right. The confessional. That's where the really interesting secrets are poured out.' Snobby grinned. 'I can see you're shocked, laddie. Supposed to be secret, isn't it? But think of it like this: there's this man—I have one in mind, but don't think you'll ever learn who—who goes into the Church purely and simply for what he can get out of it. Purely, simply and solely. Not an ounce of religious feeling in his whole make-up. He likes the good things of life, and this is his way of getting them—and a nice little bit of power to boot. From the beginning he knows that one of his ways will be using the confessional. I tell you, it's the most brilliant wheeze I ever knew.'

'You mean—blackmail?' Gordon stuttered.

''Course I mean blackmail. Used very, very discriminatingly. Which means it's a slow starter. When you're parish priest of Little Wittering-on-the-Wallop you don't try to blackmail Mary Sykes because she's sleeping with the local publican. Oh no—you take it slowly, get the notice of your superiors, emphasize that for you it's the *urban* parishes that present the real challenges to Christianity in the modern world, take up all the fashionable causes—famine, apartheid, battered wives. And little by little you get to the sort of parish, the sort of position, where you've got the real villains, and the people with things in their lives that are worth hiding.'

'Say London,' said Gordon.

'Say London,' agreed Snobby, 'though you needn't think you're going to get any more out of me than that.'

'But what's the point? What's all the blackmail money going to be spent on?'

'High living, indulged in very discreetly, and in out-of-the-way places: the Azores, Curaçao, the Æolian islands.'

Again there was that tiny click, as something fell into place. Somewhere in his notes there was a reference to a 'tiny community' of religious brothers in the Azores, to which Bishop Bannerman had often gone in retreat. Also to periods of solitary prayer, on Lipari . . .

'What was your "in" on all this?' Gordon asked, in his con-man-of-the-world manner. 'How do you come to know so much about it?'

'Oh, I was the collector. I wasn't one of the faith—that wouldn't have done at all—but he'd got something on me, never mind what, from someone who was. I collected the dibs, handed it over intact, and collected my percentage. Miserable little percentage it was too, but it all added up. No, it was a beautiful scheme, and I was proud of my part in it—profitable and risk-free. Or so I thought.'

'Not?'

'Well, my part was safe enough. You don't catch me taking any risks in a simple matter of picking up a parcel of ten-pound notes. Piece of cake, as I'm sure you know. On the other hand, the Bish—my religious friend—well, I'm afraid he overplayed his hand.'

'Went for the really big villains?'

'Something like that, though not quite in the way you mean. Now, in this bloke's parish—we'll call it a parish—there were all sorts of villains, big, medium and small, from pimps to company directors, but naturally among the ones he knew best were the Mafia mob.'

'Of course. But would they come to Confession?'

'Some of 'em. Very devout little shysters, some of 'em. So he'd hear all about the rackets involving the Iti restaurants, the fruit and veg markets, not to mention some of the fall-out from the Calvi affair, and the Banco Ambrosi-how's-yer-father. All very intriguing and profitable. And in among the rest, another little tit-bit. What that was precisely, I don't claim to know. Mostly I never *did* know. But the Mafia guy he got it from was a hard little pimp in Hackney, and I'd guess he'd been a hard little pimp in Palermo before that, so whatever it was, it was probably sexual. If it'd been something bigger he might have twigged . . .'

'So there was an Italian connection, was there? Hence Venice.'

'Oh, there was an Italian connection all right. Though of course at Venice, at this 'ere conference I attended in an unofficial capacity, there were holy-rollers from all over, as well as C. of E., Methodists, Baptists, everything except the Reverend Ian Paisley, all making out they were matey as hell and brothers in Christ. It was all very affecting, if you didn't listen to what they was saying behind each other's backs. O' course, I was just there on a package tour—'

'To collect the loot.'

'That's it. The trouble was, in Italy I was a bit of a fish out of water.' Snobby shook his head. 'Or so the B—so my reverend bloke thought. He made a plan for picking up the loot, made it himself, and I was too bleeding ignorant to argue against it. If I'd known about gondoliers . . .'

'Gondoliers?'

'I mean, all I knew about was honeymoon couples steered through the canals by a bloke with a pole who needed a shave and sang '*O Sole mio*'. I didn't know they were the biggest pimps and petty crooks in the business, and had been going back centuries, ever since they built that place on stilts.'

'I suppose it was asking for a double-cross.'

'Too right it was. Added to the fact that Mario, the punter *my* bloke employed, had a mother from Messina, and contacts with all the underworld characters in Venice and on the mainland, all the way down to sunny Sicily.'

'What went wrong?'

'Everything. Every-bloody-thing. Oh, the Iti Bishop came along—'

'Italian Bishop?'

'That's right. Him that my bloke had got the juicy little piece of information about, from the hard little crook in Hackney. He came along with his packet of ten-thousand-lira notes, and left it under the seat at the gondolier's end, just as he'd been told to in the note, and as I'd arranged with this Mario. Then I took my romantic little trip round the back canals, feeling a right berk, since I hadn't got anyone to hold 'ands with, not even a gay vicar. And then we went out into the lagoon and I transferred the package to my little briefcase—all as ordered, though somehow I didn't feel happy about it even then.'

'I suppose you were followed when you got back to dry land?'

'Must've been. And very cleverly too, because I know all the wheezes an English follerer will get up to. Naturally I didn't go straight to my bloke and say "Here's the loot". I went up and down these dark little streets and alleyways, stopped for a cappuchino, stopped for a plate of spaghetti, though I got most of it down my shirt-front. Must've been pretty conspicuous, looking back on it, because I'm not the type to carry a briefcase. Eventually, as per arrangement, I went into this scruffy bar, went to make a phone call, and dropped the parcel. My bloke, in civvies, went in immediately after, and hey presto it went into *his* brief-case. Trouble was, I wasn't followed any longer. He was. Then it was child's play to find out which hotel room he was in, and who he was. So from then on his fate was sealed.'

'His . . . fate?'

'Well, it's obvious, isn't it? Mind you, he made it easier for them himself. He'd palled up with his victim, him who was Bishop of this big town in Sicily which shall be nameless. Oh, right palsy-walsy they were, swapping jokes in Latin and I don't know what. Gave my bloke a good laugh, and that nice little feeling of power to boot—for as long as it lasted. He was in this Iti Bishop's room when he died.'

'When he had his heart attack?'

Snobby, well launched into his story, was oblivious to Gordon's mistake: so far he had not mentioned any such thing as a heart attack.

'Whatever you care to call it. Sharing a bottle of Corvo they was, a nice thick Sicilian red, in the Italian Bish's hotel room. And what does he do, this Bish, when my bloke falls down and starts eating the carpet? Does he ring the hotel Reception and say "Get me the hotel doctor"? Oh no he does not. He rings a buddy-pal, practising in Venice, brought up in the same little village on the slopes of Mount Etna. No problems about a certificate from *him*. What's the betting he was alerted in advance, eh?'

'You're not saying this bishop . . . *murdered* your man?' said Gordon, aghast. Snobby sat back in his chair and looked at him pityingly.

'You haven't understood a word I've been saying, have you? That's the whole point: they were two of a kind. They'd both gone into the Church for the same reason. That Bish was the Mafia's spiritual arm back in their home island. Confessions heard daily and passed straight on. Once he knew that his blackmailer was a priest, he knew exactly how he'd got on to him, and exactly what to do.' Snobby pushed his beer-mug away and felt for his scarf. 'Which leads me to my final words of advice to you tonight: there's no con so brilliant that two people can't think it up. And if two people running the same con bump into each other—wait for the explosion.'

He pushed back his chair and got up, but as he did so he

caught sight of Gordon's troubled expression, and seemed as if he was seeing the real man for the first time. He sat down again and looked at him seriously.

'It's fair bowled you over, hasn't it?' he said. 'You're a serious chap at heart, aren't you? Sympathetic too. People must talk to you, I shouldn't mind betting. You ever thought of going in for the Church?'

THE OXFORD WAY OF DEATH

St Pothinus's Hall is not one of the most distinguished colleges of the University of Oxford. Its academic record is frankly deplorable—a fact in which many of the dons take a twisted kind of pride. Nor is it one of the younger and livelier colleges. I myself, at forty-seven, am the second youngest of the Fellows. The vast majority are well into their sixties, or older. I once saw one of them reading over a list of the members of the Russian or Chinese politburo, with their ages, and chuckling so much he blew snuff all around the Senior Common Room. But compared to more normal institutions we are very old indeed. It has happened twice in the last year that a student would begin to read his weekly essay to a normally comatose old gentleman, only to find on concluding his piece that he had been reading for some time to a corpse. One of the young gentlemen to whom this happened let out a howl of horror and ran amok into Burton's Quad, screaming and tearing his hair. The other retrieved his books from the floor around him, placed his essay back in its folder, and went and had a quiet word with Jenkyns the porter. His conduct was much approved.

On the evening this all starts, I sat at High Table and looked around at my fellow Fellows (that is the sort of joke they like), and thought what a pathetic lot they all were. Wrinkled, bald, shrivelled, having trouble with dentures, respiration and prostate glands. With some old people you can say, in effect: 'Well, at least they've had a good life—' or an interesting or exciting one. But the lives of these dons made A. E. Housman's, by comparison, an existence jam-packed with incident. The Senior Common Room was still chuckling about a brief and unsuccessful fling our Mr

Peddie (Divinity) had had with a lady don at St Anne's. And that was back in 1934.

So anyway, there we all sat. Macnaughton, the Master, Peddie of the brief fling, Hugo Carmody (History), Pritchard-Jones (Medicine), Wittling (Classics) and the rest who play little part in this story, and who shall be left nameless. And myself, Peter Borthwick (English). Oh yes —and Auberon Smythe, the one who is younger than I. Auberon was elected in 1970, and at the interview he looked sober, discreet, well-washed. He came, we knew, from a minor public school, as we all did. When he arrived to take up residence six months later he had hair a foot long, wore kaftans, was into drugs, revolution and the gay scene, and used language that hadn't been heard at High Table since the eighteenth century. We were properly conned. Twelve years or so had tamed him, as it had most of his generation, but he was still spoken of as our Big Mistake.

As we were spooning the last of the cabinet pudding into our mouths (St Pothinus's is not renowned for its kitchen either), the Master launched himself, as was inevitable, into the subject of the next meeting of the Senior Common Room, to take place the following week. These little excitements in our lives cast long shadows before them.

'A busy time is ahead of us, I fear,' he began, in that disagreeable chainsaw voice of his which nevertheless had a certain authority, and ensured silence when he raised it above its normal whine. 'And a long meeting too. For a start there is the question of Admissions for next year.'

All the old gentlemen around him sighed. If they had their way there would be no Admissions. No more undergraduates. They had a vague sense that two hundred years ago this would have been possible, and that they lived in a degenerate age.

'No problem, surely, about Admissions,' said Peddie, as the port began to go round. 'They all come up and take the scholarship exams, and then we give the places to the sons of Old Boys as usual.'

'You forget,' neighed the Master, 'that the Old Boys are not producing many sons. Not *enough*.'

'No. Hardly a philoprogenitive lot,' said Wittling, with his horrid laugh like twenty French horns doing the prelude to *Der Rosenkavalier*.

'We could always give the places to the best applicants,' I said cautiously, for new ideas are not welcome at Potty's.

'I know what that means!' yelped Peddie, wagging an accusing finger. 'You want brains! *Brains!* Ha!'

'Besides,' said Pritchard-Jones seriously, 'it would mean reading their scholarship papers.'

'What are you talking about, EH?' bellowed Hugo Carmody from the foot of the table.

'Admissions,' I shouted back.

'Well, really!' said Hugo Carmody with a knowing wink. He is quite infuriating. He was a friend of Waugh and Acton and people back in the 'twenties, but if he was a dog then, he certainly has had his day by now. He uses his deafness as a weapon, and when we shout at him he invariably seems to turn what we say in his mind into something indecent, making us feel like smutty schoolboys. To shut him up the Master proposed a toast.

'Our benefactor, the poet-priest Heatherington,' he neighed.

More priest than poet, more gentleman than priest, more bonviveur and hanger of poachers and discontented peasantry than gentleman. We drank the health of Edmund Heatherington (1711–1779), whose entry in the *Oxford Companion to English Literature* runs to one and a half lines. It was due to the happy accident of his having died immediately after writing the one will (of some thirty) which disinherited both his son and his daughter simultaneously that the college was rolling in money. We repeated his name in hushed tones, and sipped, reverently.

'Then,' said the Master, 'there is the question of Elections.'

'What are you talking about—EH?' yelled Carmody again.

'About ele . . . about appointing new Fellows,' I shouted back.

'Really!' sniggered Carmody. 'Whatever next?'

We all sighed.

'There are of course two places to fill, due to the untimely deaths of poor Purvis and Matheson,' resumed the Master. St Pothinus's is the only place in the world where death at 76 and 81 could be described as untimely. 'It has been suggested to me by the Vice-Chancellor that this time we should make an all-out effort—'

There was a sigh. He had lost his audience already. That phrase had put them all off.

'—to appoint somebody younger. To ensure the future of the college, as he put it.'

He looked around sardonically. Everyone looked bewildered.

'What frightful balderdash,' said Peddie, looking from face to face, seemingly quite confident that not only he, but all of us, would be blessed with eternal life on earth.

'We could make another Big Mistake,' muttered Pritchard-Jones, in the sort of mutter designed to call cattle home on the hills of North Wales.

'Oh God,' said Auberon Smyth, 'when will I graduate to being just a Little Mistake?'

'I told the Vice-Chancellor,' said the Master, satisfied with our reactions, 'I fear with a touch of asperity, that the cult of the young cut no ice with us, and would not be allowed to destroy the traditional ethos of St Pothinus's. No, indeed! Nevertheless, there are these elections. We have to have a new Fellow in French. You know my opinion of studying *mod*ern languages at a uni*ve*rsity, but there it is:

the Fellowship is vacant. And then, perhaps more difficult, there is the Fellowship in Ancient Persian . . .'

The Fellowship in Ancient Persian had been held by Harold Purvis, whose death had sent his one pupil screaming into Burton Quad. Since his death his pupil had been as lacking in tuition as he undoubtedly was in *savoir faire*, since there was only one such Fellowship in the University. Not surprisingly. Many were the years when Purvis managed to attract not one single undergraduate pupil.

'I don't see the difficulty,' suddenly chirped up Wittling. There was an edge to his voice that I knew and did not like. It meant mischief. Wanton, senile malice.

'Oh?' whinnied the Master. 'You have a candidate?'

'*I* don't have a candidate. I know there will *be* a candidate. There is only *one* person in Britain qualified for the position, and that person will certainly apply, positions in that field being by no means plenteous.'

'No, indeed: we are nearly, very nearly unique,' breathed the Master, with immense satisfaction. 'I hope this is not a *young* person, Wittling?'

'Thirty-two, I believe, Master.'

'Oh dear. *Very* young indeed. It seems the decision will be taken out of our hands. You say there is virtually no alternative?'

'No, Master,' said Wittling, with what was obviously some secret satisfaction. 'And I'm told that Sandowa Bulewa is brilliant, absolutely brilliant.'

There was a moment's silence.

'What was that name?' bellowed Carmody (who could hear when he wanted to) from the end of the table. 'Don't tell me it's some damned foreigner, for God's sake.'

'No, no. Born in Britain. Quite the homemade article.'

'But the name,' insisted the Master. 'It's not—'

'Not English, no. Tanganyikan, I believe, or whatever they call the place these days. Mother was Kenyan, I'm told.'

'Then he's not . . . you're not telling us—'

'Black. Black as your hat. Yes, Master.'

'Gracious heavens!' said the Master. 'Whatever next?'

'It's a retreat to barbarism,' said Peddie.

'Something must be done,' neighed the Master, at his most imperative. 'I feel the modern world has suddenly rapped most brutally at our door.'

'Personally,' said Auberon Smythe, 'I rather fancy the idea.'

It was all too clear what form the idea took for Smythe. Exclusively sexual. He was imagining a splendid black lover. But I felt I had to back him up.

'If we refused to appoint the man,' I said, 'we would certainly be in contravention of the Race Relations Act.'

'Heavens above,' said Pritchard-Jones. 'What's that?'

I explained at some length, ending up: 'If we have no adequate grounds for refusing him the Fellowship, he could certainly appeal to the Tribunal.'

'Admirably expounded,' cut in Wittling as I concluded, and now his voice had a suggestion of real mirth which absolutely made the blood run cold. 'But I must correct you, pedantically no doubt, on one little detail. You have been referring to Sandowa Bulewa throughout as "he". However the correct personal pronoun would be the third person *feminine*: "she", dear boy, "she".' And he chortled that awful laugh that sounded like whooping, Straussian French horns.

'But that's splendid. She's not elig . . .' The Master's voice faded away. This third shock left him looking as if he had heard the opening of Beethoven's Fifth played by massed Midlands brass bands and amplified a thousand-fold. He looked at Wittling with outraged reproach.

For the powers that be at St Pothinus's had been caught in a trap of their own devising. Some years before, when all the Oxford colleges were changing their statutes, recruiting female dons, even admitting women students, we had, under strong pressure from the university authorities, declared all our senior appointments open to female applicants. We (or rather *they*) had done this on the clear understanding that nothing whatever was to come of it. I distinctly remembered Wittling at the meeting chuckling his horrible chuckle and saying: 'We declare them eligible, and we just don't appoint any. He-he-he!' It had seemed to most of them an awfully jolly wheeze at the time. I had no doubt that the Master was remembering this now.

'Wittling,' he said. 'This is at least in part your doing. I shall rely on you to find some way of getting us out of it.'

'Out of it?' crowed Wittling. 'Why should I want to get us out of it? Jolly good idea. Pretty young black thing. Brighten the place up. Spruce us up a bit too. I believe she's a very lively little thing—modern, and all that. What's the phrase?—"with it". He-he-he.'

'Then what on earth is she studying Ancient Persian for?' demanded Pritchard-Jones.

'I'm told she has a Protestant Mission background from her parents. Went up to Cambridge to study theology. Got into New Testament Greek. Went on from there. Lost her religion, but proved a—he-he-he—whizzkid in ancient languages. Studied Persian at the Sorbonne.'

'Heavens above!' bellowed Carmody. 'It doesn't seem possible. What are gels coming to?'

'I have it! I have it!' shrieked the Master, a rare and terrifying smile wreathing his aged face. 'The Fellowship can be changed. Its terms can be altered. We can turn it into a Fellowship in Geography. Or Spanish. Or Comparative Something-or-other. That,' he concluded triumphantly, 'is possible under the terms of Edmund Heatherington's will. The endower of the Fellowship.'

'Quite,' said Wittling. 'It is possible. *Providing the Fellows are unanimous in desiring the change.*'

'Well?' Magisterially.

'They will not be unanimous. I myself do not desire
the change. I must uphold the importance of the dead
languages.' He sniggered. 'I have no doubt that Mr . . . er,
Dr' (sneer) 'Smythe, being a *modern* young man, will not
wish the nature of the Fellowship to be changed in order to
exclude a member of the female sex.'

Now Auberon Smythe is one of the few homosexuals who
seem genuinely to dislike women. But he too felt himself
caught in one of Wittling's fork-like traps.

'No. No, of course not,' he muttered.

'And you, Borthwick,' continued Wittling, turning to me,
'a liberal young fellow like you would naturally like to see
the College open to women.'

'Of course,' I said, with a touch of priggishness that
comes, I think, from my Scottish ancestry. 'I would certainly
be against changing the terms of the Fellowship if that were
the motive.'

'Three dissenting!' said Wittling, in tones of triumph.
'Not a chance of a unanimous vote, Master. Not a chance!'

It was death to the Master's hopes. All his powers of
command seemed to have left him. He summoned Jenkyns
the porter, who led him from table, back to his Residence.
As he staggered off, I saw him removing his dentures,
something he only does in public when he is very upset.
The rest of us broke up raggedly, and the evening concluded
in less of an alcoholic fugg than usual.

I am not quite sure why Wittling did all this. I'm convinced that when he suggested altering the statutes to admit
women he had no such far-sighted project as this in mind.
Nor, of course, did he have any particular love of women
as such. I'm sure no tingling of lust warmed his aged loins,
or had, since about the time of *Chu Chin Chow*. I think it
was just mischief. That's the trouble when you get older.
Either you think you're immortal, and this gives you a
godlike carelessness of consequences, or else you know you'll
soon be dead, and won't have to put up with the results of

your mischief. If the latter was Wittling's calculation, he was all too soon to be proved right.

In the week that followed I absented myself from College as much as possible, for squabbling geriatrics are hardly congenial companions. My only insight into how things were going I obtained one evening when, after a late tutorial, I went over to the buttery bar to have a beer before going home for dinner. The door stood open, and I heard the booming voice of Hugo Carmody.

'Well, I don't know if the Master has any plans, but I'm damned sure *some*thing's got to be done.' I lingered in the twilight outside the door. 'If only we could *get* something on them.'

'Absolutely,' I heard, in the sharp voice of Peddie.

'Smythe would be easy, what? Threaten to go to the Police about his boyfriends.'

'That wouldn't do. It's not illegal any more.'

'What? Not illegal? Good heavens! I must stop slipping Higgins five-pound notes.'

Higgins was Carmody's scout. He was reaching retirement age, so he wouldn't greatly miss his five-pound notes. There was silence for a moment.

'Then there's Borthwick. Not much to be got on him. A somewhat *dim* personality, what?'

'His wife is sleeping with the milkman, you know,' came the thin, malicious voice of Peddie. They chuckled about this like crazy.

'But all the Fellows' wives sleep with one or other of the roundsmen. I always said that marriage doesn't *do*. And really it's hardly a *lever*.'

They subsided into silence, and I made a bustling entrance. I had a quick beer, and resolved to be home more in the mornings.

Nothing much happened that I knew of until the night before the Senior Common Room meeting. My wife was at an Oxfam gathering, she said, and I was forced to eat in

Hall. Dinner was uneventful but unpleasant. No one was talking to Wittling, so he was forced to talk to me and Smythe. Given the choice I preferred Pritchard-Jones, who was at least inoffensive, or even Hugo Carmody, because I was always hoping to get out of him details of a trip he made to Paris with Waugh in 1924. But Wittling it was, and we were forced to put up with his crackling malice, his sly self-satisfaction, his trumpeted chortlings. After dinner we adjourned as usual to the Senior Common Room. I poured myself a second glass of port, and Wittling did the same. Smythe took a hard slug of whisky, and the master took coffee and brandy. Wittling stood by the mantelpiece, and though the rest of us wanted to cluster round the fire, we none of us wanted to be too near him.

'St Pothinus!' said the Master, who had placed himself in the centre of the room. We all toasted the patron saint of the College (dead at ninety, in a dungeon), and then the Master fixed Wittling with an eye, bleary, but designed to threaten and command.

'Well, Wittling, we're all hoping to hear you've changed your mind.'

'Changed my mind, Master?' Innocently.

'About altering the terms of the Fellowship.'

'Oh, *that*—' (dismissively, as if the matter had passed completely out of his head). 'No, Master, I fear that my opinions on that subject are very much as they were last week.'

'I see, I see-e-e. So, to satisfy a foolish whim, to enjoy a bit of wilful trouble-making, you are prepared to jeopardize the best traditions of St Pothinus.'

'What did Winston Churchill say about the traditions of the Navy? Rum, sodomy and the lash? I suppose you could say that St Pothinus's were port, sodomy and the third-class honours degree. Personally, I believe traditions should be evaluated empirically. The obsolete ones discarded, what?'

'What you are proposing,' snapped Peddie, 'is a craven concession to the spirit of modernity.'

'Concession?' chortled Wittling. 'Not at all. I propose welcoming it in! A breath of fresh air from the contemporary scene. Apropos of which, I have a *picture*—' he skipped, chuckling and snuffling, over to his briefcase in a corner by the door—'a snapshot, I think you call it, of the young lady herself, some years ago, taken when she was performing in the Cambridge Footlights Review ... Ah, here it is.'

He produced from his case an old, slightly brown copy of the *Sun* newspaper, and we clustered round to view a picture of a distinctly handsome black girl, in leopardskin briefs, apparently topless, clutching a microphone in the centre of a stage, swaying her hips and crooning into it.

'My word!' said Carmody, 'I suppose that was taken after she lost her faith.'

None of the rest of us could think of anything more adequate to say.

'There,' said Wittling triumphantly, looking around at us and thrusting the photograph at the Master who was wandering over from the fireplace. 'Now you can see that Miss Bulewa will certainly provide something different in the College, what? Can't see anyone paying to see us topless, eh? Except perhaps Dr Smythe in some dubious Soho locale.' He pottered back towards the fire. 'No, this *is* going to be a bit of a change, isn't it? I hope she fits in. Do you feel she will? Don't you sometimes feel you've got into a bit of a rut here, all of you? That life is lacking in zest? Needs a bit of spice. Suddenly our lives are going to acquire a whole new flavour.'

He picked up his glass of port, and drank triumphantly. Suddenly an expression of horror, or rage, crossed his face, which set in a terrible grimace. His hand dropped the glass and went to his throat, a strangled cry escaped him, and he crashed forward on to the hearthrug.

'Dear me,' said the Master. 'Mr Wittling appears to be unwell.'

I was down on the hearthrug beside him, pulling open his dinner jacket, feeling his pulse. No one else moved. I didn't need long.

'He's dead,' I said.

'How unfortunate,' said the Master, taking a fortifying sip of his brandy. 'Struck down in his prime. In the midst of life . . . The ways of Providence are strange.'

'Providence, my foot!' I said brutally. 'You saw how he died. He's been poisoned.'

'Mr Borthwick! Mis-ter Borthwick! What an extraordinary suggestion! Most improper. You've been reading too many books by—what's that *thriller* writer?—Mr Wilkie Collins.'

'Can't you smell it? Almonds. It must have been in the port.'

'Gad! Founder's Port,' said Hugo Carmody.

'I can't smell a thing,' said Peddie. 'Look—I'm drinking port. It's perfectly all right.' And he downed his drink.

'I'm drinking port too,' I said. 'It must have been put in his *glass*. He'd already drunk half of it. It must have been put in his glass while we were all looking at his damned newspaper.'

'Come, come, Mr Borthwick, let us not lose grip of our logic,' said the Master in his unpleasant, silken whine. 'If we were all looking at his newspaper, none of us could have put anything in his glass.'

'One of us must have held back,' I said, crinkling my forehead with effort. 'One of us wasn't there.' I had a vision of the paper being thrust at the Master as he came from the direction of the fireplace. I looked at him, and he stared unwaveringly back.

'We were all gaping at it, far as I remember,' said Pritchard-Jones. 'Handsome filly.'

'Quite,' said the Master. 'We were all over that side of

the room. Now let us forget this frivolous suggestion, and—'

'No doctor on earth is going to sign a death certificate, Master,' I said. 'There'll have to be an autopsy.'

'I'm sure Dr Pritchard-Jones will have no hesitation in signing the necessary formalities,' said the Master smoothly.

'Pritchard-Jones? He hasn't practised medicine since before penicillin was invented.'

'I believe you are eligible to sign the necessary forms?' inquired the Master in his high whinny, turning to Pritchard-Jones.

''Course I am. Most uncalled-for remark. Offensive.'

'I believe there *was* some history of heart trouble, wasn't there?'

'Think there was. Know he went to his doctor last week. I can square it with Smithers. Man's practically senile. Needn't be any question of a post-mortem.'

'There we are, then. That's all quite clear. There need be no question.'

'Master, even if you have a certificate,' I explained patiently, 'no undertaker is going to bury that corpse without getting a police clearance first.'

'Why on earth not?'

'Well—look!' I turned over the corpse. The face of Mr Wittling, blue, and twisted into a hideous grimace of torment that seemed to drag his wrinkled skin tight over his aged skull, gazed horrifyingly up at us.

'Well, he was nobody's idea of a dreamboat at the best of times,' said Auberon Smythe.

'I've no doubt Lockitt will not make any trouble,' said the Master. 'We'll get *old* Lockitt. Not the boy, he's a fusser. Old Lockitt is quite as old as any of us, and nearly blind. He's very understanding. He won't want to lose us—we've been one of their most regular customers, over the years.'

'You are covering up! You are accessories after a murder!'

'Covering up? Really, Mr Borthwick. You'll be suggesting next that I committed murder myself.'

He looked at me, and I, weakly, looked down at the floor.

'Well, how do I know that you didn't? How do I know that you're not all in it? Pritchard-Jones, what poison is it that smells like almonds?'

'Don't know, m'boy. Have to look it up in m'books.'

'It must have been brought here.' I looked desperately round the room. 'Look! Here it is.' I picked up from one of the side tables a tiny glass phial. 'This is how it was brought.'

'No doubt it contained some medicament that poor Wittling was taking for his heart,' said the Master.

'He did not have heart trouble,' I said. 'We'd have heard about it endlessly if he had. Smythe: you can see what's happening, can't you? Can I rely on you to support me?'

'Fight your own battles,' said Auberon Smythe, making for the door. 'I've no love for the police, believe me. As far as I'm concerned, I went straight to my rooms after Hall. Haven't been near the SCR all evening. 'Bye, duckies.'

'What did he say?' roared Carmody, but we ignored him.

'Right,' I said. 'If I have to fight my own battles, so be it.' I marched over to the telephone, recently installed in the SCR as a concession to the times. 'If you won't listen to me, perhaps you'll listen to the police.'

'The police?' neighed the Master. 'Really, Mr Borthwick, if we can't settle a little matter like this without calling in outside authorities, what has become of academic freedom?'

I didn't deign to answer, and was just beginning to dial when the Master spoke again, with that authoritative undertone to his whine that always got his point across.

'Mr Borthwick, you really must be careful, you know. I don't *think* you have quite thought this thing through.'

'What do you mean?' I demanded.

'Well, let us say, for argument's sake, that we are all "in it", as you put it a moment ago. It will be very easy, will it not, for us, all of us, to inform the police of a most unfortunate altercation, really quite violent, that took place last week between you and poor Wittling—'

'Altercation? There was no altercation. I hardly spoke to the man if I could help it.'

'Precisely. Your hostility was well known to us. And in an enclosed community such as our own, it is well known how little things can fester, and become great ones. There was that altercation, as I say. On the subject of—what was it?—Milton's debt to Virgil. Yes, I think that was it. We all heard it, of course. Now, would the police believe your story, of a collusion between a large number of elderly and impeccably respectable academic gentlemen to murder one of their colleagues? Or would they not rather accept our unanimous view that you—your mind unhinged, perhaps, by the notorious infidelities of your wife—had a brainstorm and decided to do away with a colleague with whom you were publicly on the worst of terms?'

'That's ridiculous.'

'Or say our splendid British police discovered that this was the work of one man. Say Mr Peddie. Say Mr Carmody. Say, even, myself. Leaving the rest of the SCR intact. You have been so taken up, I fear, with the terms of the Fellowship in Ancient Persian that you have forgotten the terms of your own Fellowship . . .'

'My own—?'

'As some of us here remember, when the Jeremy Collier Fellowship in English was established, English was still a comparatively new university subject. Many of us hoped it would go away. So, in their wisdom, the governing fellows made this Fellowship renewable every five years.'

'But that's just a formali—'

'*It has been hitherto*. Quite. We have been generous, as is our habit. However, the Fellowship comes up for renewal, does it not, *next year*. I think you may find that the SCR will not take kindly to the idea of renewing the Fellowship of one who has been responsible for arraigning one of their colleagues on a capital charge.'

'Damned bad form,' said Carmody.

'Quite,' said Peddie.

'Quite,' said all of them, sounding like a flock of ducks in St James's Park.

'You wouldn't dare,' I said, but my voice sounded hollow.

'I think you would find that to get a job at your time of life is far from easy. A cold academic wind is blowing, is it not, Borthwick? Positions are being abolished, rather than created, I believe. I'm told that even in the Colonies the universities are no longer the refuge for Oxonians that they once were. And though you are a great *reader*, Borthwick, you are hardly a prolific *writer*, are you? Isn't that what they want these days? Acres of little papers on this and that? It doesn't bear thinking about, does it, Borthwick? One of the great army of three million unemployed.'

I took my hand slowly from the telephone. He had me over a bubbling cauldron of boiling oil. When threatened where it hurts most, our jobs and our pockets, we liberal intellectuals do not hesitate. Or rather, we hesitate, because that is in our natures, but in the end . . .

I took a symbolic step away from the telephone.

'Splendid!' neighed the Master, rubbing his hands. 'I felt quite sure you'd see you'd been mistaken. Sad that the death of a respected and valued colleague should have been disfigured in this way. Now I fear I must to the Residence, to set in motion the necessary formalities.' He looked around the room carefully. He took up the little phial from the table, and hurled it into the fire. Then he took the copy of the *Sun* and placed it carefully in his briefcase.

'I shall ring Lockitt's, talk to the old man. I'll tell him to bring along a certificate for you to sign, Pritchard-Jones. Perhaps you would stay here too, Peddie, to see if there's anything else? The rest of us can go, I think. Borthwick, we'll quite understand if you are too upset to attend tomorrow's meeting: you have taken the death of your friend very hard, we can all see that. I shall propose to change the terms of the Heatherington Fellowship to one in Chinese. I think Wittling would have approved, with his concern for the older languages. And it will show that we in Potty's can, in our small way, adapt ourselves to the new patterns of the modern world.'

And that's how it turned out. We appointed two new Fellows. One was a Chinese scholar of great age and Buddha-like inscrutability, the other an elderly Winchester schoolmaster who was having disciplinary problems. They fitted in very well. Life in college goes on pretty much as before. For a time I did not care to go to High Table. I dined constantly at home, driving my wife to a frenzy of irritation. Even when I started to eat in Hall again, I avoided the port. But Time takes the edge off most things. Now I take my glass of Founder's Port with the rest, with scarcely a thought.

It's amazing what we liberal intellectuals can take in our strides, when we set our minds to it.

DAYLIGHT ROBBERY

In any league table of Britain's stately homes, Hardacre Hall would not figure in the top ten. Nor in the second ten, nor yet in the ten after that. Only in a list of the least stately homes open to the public could Hardacre be expected to be given any prominence. People wondered why Lord Woolmington bothered to open it at all, for the receipts could hardly recompense him for his trouble, but the fact is that it gave him and Lady Woolmington an interest, and something to talk about. 'That chappie with the dentures—insurance salesman, wouldn't y'say?' Woolmington would chuckle at the end of his day's activity of showing the occasional visitors round in ones and twos. 'And did you notice that frightful woman's hat?'

Lady Woolmington, Cissie, sat in the entrance hall in an old print frock, a little electric fire by her be-socked ankles, and took the money—a pound a time for adults, 50p for children, pensioners and the unemployed. When the money was safely in her possession, she would say: 'Tours of the house go on the hour and the half-hour,' and the visitor was compelled to mooch around the hall for anything up to twenty-five minutes, watched over by a dyspeptic moose over the main door, which had one eye falling disconcertingly out of its socket. Almost never did anyone else come during this wait, and Lady Woolmington would make bright remarks such as 'This rain's keeping people away,' or 'In this heat people want to be outside.' The implication that normally the house was athrong with tourists was not one the visitors ever tested. Visitors never came back.

Hardacre Hall was, in truth, only the pokey dower house where generations of dowager Lady Woolmingtons had been shunted off by their newly ennobled sons. True it was built in 1818, but it only proved that inelegant and inconvenient domestic architecture was not suddenly born with the Victorian age, any more than prudery or hypocrisy was.

The Woolmingtons had been country squires and baronets in Pendleshire for two centuries, and had been raised to a barony in 1901, for the first Lord Woolmington had lent Edward VII a large sum of money to cover a gambling debt when he was Prince of Wales. It would, in truth, have been better for the family if he had repaid the loan, for shortly after the First World War they had been forced to sell Woolmington Hall to a speculative builder, who had pulled it down and built half-timbered semis. The Lords Woolmington had retired to Hardacre, adding Hall to its name, and had been there ever since, dwindling.

Promptly on the hour Lord Woolmington would potter in. He would go around shaking hands with the waiting party of two or three, saying 'Rotten day, isn't it?' or 'Gardens need rain, what?' Then the tour would commence.

The rooms open to the public—the dining-room, the drawing-room, the green bedroom and the library—left the minds of the more discriminating visitor boggling as to what the unseen rooms could contain. Bumbling along through the dark and ill-decorated rooms, crammed with undistinguished or positively decrepit furniture, Lord Woolmington would seize arbitrarily and unpredictably on some article or other and proffer it before the visitor's listless gaze.

'That's a knife,' he would proclaim, after a lunge at the mantelpiece had yielded a shoddy little tourist souvenir from the Iberian peninsula. 'Sent by m'cousin Maud from Oporto. Family tradition says it's Toledo steel. Shouldn't think so m'self.' For favoured visitors he would add: 'Retired there for her health, m'cousin Maud, so she said. *We* thought it was for the port.'

So the tour continued. Here was the second Baroness's work basket—'just as she left it'. Here in a glass case was a pike caught by the seventh Baronet: 'not specially large, but it was practically the only time he caught anything at all'. He would flick his hand at an old candelabrum in a dusty corner, in the holders of which were dried arrangements done by his cousin Sylvia in 1957: 'Candlesticks. That sort of thing appeal to you?' Here was a picture of the first Baron in his 1911 Coronation robes; here was the present Lady Woolmington, before her marriage, doing her debutante's curtsey before Edward VIII, he looking positively lethal in his boredom. The second Baron's saddle and the first Baroness's false front did not add significantly to the interest of the place, nor did the library, which contained bound volumes of *Punch* from 1840 until they could no longer afford to take it, a large collection of old green Penguins, and the odd copy of *Men Only*.

In the middle of this fascinating collection of forgettabilia, Lord Woolmington's mind was often distracted by things of even less import. 'There's last week's *Radio Times*,' he would mutter, and the visitor would shoot a glance there as if it were a collector's item. Or: 'Don't tell me Ben's done his business by the coal scuttle,' he would fret, and the visitor would keep his distance, since Ben had already been identified as the old sheepdog, faithful of heart if incontinent of bowel, who accompanied every guided tour.

Sometimes in undistinguished houses the discriminating visitor's spirits are kept up by the hope of discovering some gem from an Old Master's hand. Not at Hardacre Hall. 'That's a genuine Witherspoon,' Lord Woolmington would say, darting into a dark corner. 'Friend of Whistler's, y'know.' The nearest any member of the family had come to being painted by a 'name' had been when John Singer Sargent was engaged to paint the wife of the first Lord Woolmington. 'Couldn't come. Dose of the clap or some damned thing. Sent this chap Bootle instead. Came a damned sight cheaper.'

The visitor gazed for a moment at the wife of the first Baron, in pink and purple cretonne against a background of Sheffield fog, and then Lord Woolmington was away again. 'And this is an Atkinson Grimshaw. Boar Lane, Leeds. Know Leeds at all?' Only when they were nearly back at the entrance hall did the visitor momentarily perk up when Lord Woolmington suddenly barked: 'That's a Turner.' Only to sink when he added: 'Reproduction. Got it at the Tate Gallery Shop. Always did like Folkestone.'

At the end of the tour the victims slunk speechless away. Few attempted to tip the guide, but if one should, an American or an Arab, Lord Woolmington murmured genially, 'Quite unnecessary. Thank you very much,' and pocketed the base coin.

When the last tour had set off—if there was one—at half past five, Lady Woolmington went down to the gate and swivelled round the sign to read CLOSED FOR THE DAY. Then she ambled off to the kitchen to prepare the haddock or the lamb chops she had bought for their dinners. After dinner they watched television in the library, or played Happy Families, or sometimes Lord Woolmington walked into the village to the Woolmington Arms, where he was an honoured customer, despite the fact that, in the manner of his kind, he always accepted offers of drinks, but never made them.

It was in the Woolmington Arms that the turn in the house's fortunes was first publicly broached.

'Took twenty pounds today,' Lord Woolmington announced to Jim behind the bar. 'Can't remember when I last took that much.' Which was not surprising, for he never had. To celebrate he added: '*Best* bitter, please, Jim.'

Lord Woolmington had no notion that this was anything other than a flash in the pan. The next day's takings were down to an ordinary ten pounds, the day after to fourteen. But on Saturday they took twenty-five pounds, and the Wednesday after thirty-four. Not once in that week did they go below twenty.

'Double whisky, please, Jim,' Lord Woolmington began saying, in the Woolmington Arms.

At the end of that second week of prosperity he went to a jumble sale in Little Pemberley and bought a chamber pot, which he began displaying to visitors as the first Lady Woolmington's. 'Waterworks trouble, y'know,' he always added. One or two other things that he picked up at auctions or second-hand shops he incorporated imaginatively into the family tradition.

The fact was, Lord Woolmington and Hardacre Hall were becoming a fashionable joke. It had not happened by accident. It all came back to Edwina, Countess of Carbury, who lived at Burtlesham Towers, some twenty miles away. Pendleshire had in fact been swallowed up, during the last local government reorganization but one, and was now part of Greater Cumbershire, but the Pendleshire gentry and aristocracy were a clannish lot, and they stuck together. Thus Lady Carbury knew the Woolmingtons quite well, and thought them 'a tremendous scream'. One day she had been driven by rain to stop at the Hall with some visitors from London—journalists, for she was herself sale-room correspondent for the *Country Lady*—and Lady Woolmington had insisted on believing they had come not to call, but to take the guided tour. 'Five quid it cost me!' Lady Carbury said ruefully to her husband afterwards. But she had not been unaware that her guests had found the tour of the house gloriously risible, and had spent much of the time in the car back to Burtlesham giving spirited imitations of Lord Woolmington's dottier pronouncements and odder mannerisms.

The joke of it is,' Lady Carbury said, in the middle of her guests' mirth, 'that in among all that junk he's got the most lovely Atkinson Grimshaw.'

And her guests, most of whom had never heard of Atkinson Grimshaw, nodded wisely, until someone shrieked 'That's m'Great Aunt Flora's tea-caddy!' and the car rocked with laughter again.

The Countess's mention of Atkinson Grimshaw was a

matter—as most things were with the Countess—of pure calculation. Burtlesham Towers was a very different kind of stately home from Hardacre. It was run most efficiently by the young Earl and his Countess: it had an adventure playground and a tropical aviary, a collection of Chippendale and a fine Van Dyke, to say nothing of a Gainsborough and two Sir Thomas Lawrences. It was a house that coach parties visited, families made the object of day outings, and it advertised on railway stations throughout the North. Nevertheless, the Earl and the Countess were regrettably short of the ready, and the Countess was—in wish if not in fact—an expensive young lady who had perpetual and urgent uses for the ready. Hence, of course, her taking on the job of saleroom correspondent.

Now to sell off any of the house's real treasures was out of the question. The Earl would never have consented, and to do so would have been self-defeating, since it must lessen the appeal of the house to the public at large. In addition, all the really important pictures were part of an entail which it would have been costly and time-consuming to undo. There were, on the other hand, works by lesser hands, among them three Atkinson Grimshaws, bought by a Victorian ancestor from the Leeds artist to make less grim some of the guest bedrooms in the East Wing. These the Earl would never regret, could surely be persuaded to sell. Thus, over a few months previous to Hardacre's sudden access of visitors, there had crystallized in the Countess's mind a plan—not a criminal conspiracy, for it certainly is not criminal to increase in value one's own possessions—but a series of delicate manœuvres which would have precisely that effect.

Twice over the last year the Countess's column in the *Country Lady* had hinted that if there *was* an artist whose stock was rising, it was that fascinating late-Victorian Atkinson Grimshaw, whose atmospheric townscapes . . . fascinating experiments with light . . . and so on, and so on. It was a name, too, that the Countess continually yet delicately brought into conversations with friends on the fringes of the art world.

On the other hand, such delicate manœuverings seemed likely to have but marginal success. If, on the other hand, the campaign to boost Grimshaw's saleable value could be linked with someone . . . someone with the capacity to be a personality of some kind . . .

Thus, when those first visitors had gone, the Countess began to think about her visit to Hardacre Hall, and to conceive a strategy that was half joke, half serious. The first stage began when she started to talk at parties about Hardacre and the Woolmingtons as if they were the latest, most exquisitely *in* thing.

'Have you been to Hardacre, darling?' she would ask. 'It is the most *ab*solute scream. Woolmington himself—Wooffy —is perfectly priceless, and his tour of the house is one of *the* great comic turns of the century.'

And always, after some surprisingly vivid imitations, she would add: 'And the funny thing is, you know, that he really has this *one* thing—this quite gorgeous Atkinson Grimshaw! One of the very best specimens!'

Thus, in the manner of these things, Hardacre Hall began to be talked about, began to get visited, first by the Countess's friends, and their friends. Then, as so often happens, the fashion gradually percolated downwards, so that, as the summer wore on, people in pubs and Women's Institutes might be heard imitating 'Wooffy' Woolmington's guided tours: 'And that's a genuine Witherspoon!' someone would say, to gales of laughter. Or: 'That's m'sister's christening spoon. Traveller chappie once offered me three pounds for that, but I didn't take it.' And as often as not they would add: 'The joke of it is, he's got this absolutely marvellous Atkinson Grimshaw. You know, the Leeds artist. Don't think he realizes how good it is.'

The success of Hardacre and Lord Woolmington could

not remain merely local. The second stage of Lady Carbury's campaign would in any case have seen to that. That stage envisaged the whole thing going national. In July there was a five-minute feature on the BBC's *Look North* programme, when a very snooty young lady was rendered speechless by Lord Woolmington's rambles through the detritus of his family's history. Then the *Observer* Colour Supplement chose him for their 'A Room of my Own' series, and photographed him among the aristocratic rubble, with the Atkinson Grimshaw prominent in the background ('I'll skin you alive if you don't get that in,' the Countess had told the photographer). Soon gossip writers began to call, and though they soon found that he knew no one who was anyone outside Pendleshire, they were enchanted by his personality, and wrote cod articles about the splendours of his stately home. Everybody loves a lord, but they go quite overboard about a dotty lord. In Germany or Italy Lord Woolmington might have been locked up, or at least put in the care of some strong-minded relative. In Britain he was encouraged to speak in the House of Lords, asked to open supermarkets, put on the team of *Any Questions*.

Not that he accepted all these signifiers of fame and popularity. 'Damned cheek!' he often said, when reading through some of the requests he received. Still, some of them were very lucrative. When he went to the Woolmington Arms of an evening, he often now took Lady Woolmington with him, even bought her an elaborate and expensive cocktail that had been popular in her youth. More often there were people there who were anxious to buy drinks for them. 'Quite unnecessary . . . Thank you very much,' Wooffy would murmur.

Meanwhile the sale price of Atkinson Grimshaws began steadily yet appreciably to rise. Little ladies in crumbling Leeds terraces found that the picture that had hung over the fireplace for as long as *they* could remember was by the same artist as the picture that Lord Whatsit was always photographed in front of. A good specimen—and Grimshaw at his best was an extremely competent painter—might before all the fuss began fetch anything up to five thousand. As Grimshaws emerged from cellars and attics they failed to sate the demand for him: it grew. Seven thousand, ten thousand, twelve thousand became commonplace. 'He has been *much* underrated,' the art historians claimed, as prices soared (a case of art imitating commerce). Working behind the scenes, the Countess ensured that the Tate bought one, the Manchester Gallery another. All her visitors were sent off back south with unjunctions that they *must* stop at Leeds on the way down and see all the Grimshaws in the Leeds Gallery. And if they *could* get into the Grand Hall of the Leeds Grand Theatre, they really should seize the chance.

'It's daylight robbery,' a fellow saleroom correspondent unknowingly whispered to her, when a Grimshaw was knocked down for seventeen thousand. The Countess shrugged.

'So is a Turner for eight million, great artist though he is.'

The crucial thing, of course, was to recognize when the fad had reached its peak. She understood that some American interest had to be created in Grimshaw, but she also understood the limits of her talents, and Grimshaw's, well enough to realize that there was never going to be a Grimshaw craze in the States: he was from an unfashionable period in British art, and he seemed unadventurous and provincial beside his contemporaries the French Impressionists whom the Americans so besottedly admire. Grimshaw was never going to be bought by the Metropolitan, nor even by that snapper-up of everybody else's trifles, the Getty. Still, there were specialist galleries, dealers with whom she had contacts . . . She had a couple of little house-parties for such people, took them to Leeds and Hardacre, showed them Burtlesham's own Grimshaws. It all created a little ripple of interest among cognoscenti in the States.

It was when she was entertaining her third party of American experts that the Countess began to feel that the time was ripe for a quick kill. To leave it much longer might mean the brief revival had passed its peak. One of the Americans, the director of a gallery in the mid-West with a sizeable and intensely boring collection of late nineteenth-century American and British paintings, had begun putting out delicate feelers, in a way the Countess recognized very well. Grimshaw would add a touch of near-distinction to his undistinguished collection. He wanted to buy.

She took them over to Hardacre, of course.

'There's the most divine Grimshaw there. *Wooffy* won't sell, of course. It's about the only thing the poor darling *has* got.'

She timed it so they were just in time for the four o'clock tour.

'You have to do the tour. It's the combination of Wooffy's *price*less performance with the reactions of people to it.'

The Americans loved the tour, loved Wooffy. All of them watched him intently, treasuring up details of the perform-ance to retail to family and friends back home. When the gallery director from the mid-West lingered in front of the Atkinson Grimshaw, Lord Woolmington shoved him forward.

'Come along, come along! I want you to see this genuine Witherspoon!'

After the tour, the Americans sampled a new departure for Hardacre: tea and horrible floury currant scones made in the mornings before the house opened by Cissie Wool-mington herself, and served in the kitchen by a mentally retarded girl from the village. The Countess knew better than to sample these delights. She stayed behind to talk to Wooffy, and on an impulse of generosity said to him:

'You know, Wooffy, in three or four months' time, you ought to sell that Grimshaw. You'll get five or six times what you would have got twelve months ago, and I don't know that he might not start sliding soon.'

Then the Americans came up from the kitchen, belching bicarbonate, and they set off home. He'll bring it up on the journey home, thought the Countess, and she didn't mean Lady Woolmington's scones.

And he did. He didn't want to be pushy, or out of line, he said, but *was* there a chance that Earl Carbury might consider . . .

'You know, darling, I think he *might*. We're not really in the business of *selling* paintings, you know, but those are hardly part of the artistic treasury of the house. He'd have to be per*suade*d. I don't know what sort of sum you were thinking of offering . . . ?'

'Say sixty thousand for the three.'

'*Pounds*, I take it. With the dollar the way it is, you've got to mean pounds . . . I think you ought to be prepared to up it by five, even ten, don't you, depending on his reaction? Sixty-five thousand? Even seventy? Because I do know he'll need to be persuaded. Best all round if I don't appear in all this, don't you think? You make the offer, and I'll do what I can behind the scenes. George is a dear soul, but just a trifle stick-in-the-mud, and he has this thing about the family heritage . . .'

They had driven past the public car park, and round the drive to the front of the house. The Countess was so taken up with the conversation that she had drawn to a halt before she realized that also pulled up there were three white police cars, and that a constable was standing in the great doorway.

'My God! What's happened? Don't tell me there's been an accident in the Adventure Playground!'

She had jumped out and shouted, 'What is it? What's happened?' to the constable at the door when the figure of the Earl, red-faced but solicitous, appeared through it.

'Don't worry, darling. Don't panic. Somehow the security seems to have broken down. There's been a theft. Must have been one of the visitors.'

'Oh my God!'

'Calm down. It sounds worse than it is. They couldn't get at any of the good stuff. They've only taken the Atkinson Grimshaws, thank heavens. And I've got them insured for six thousand.'

'Y'know, I'm not at all sure I won't accept that Yank's offer,' said Wooffy Woolmington the next evening, over a final glass of Glenmuckitt malt whisky in the Hardacre sitting-room.

'I thought you would,' said Cissie, knitting peacefully, 'when you didn't say no at once.'

'Feel a bit guilty. Seems a damned shame, and damned hard on that nice little Edwina Carbury. Those damned thieves knew they'd never get away with the Van Dyke, and wouldn't be able to sell it if they did. There's been all this talk about Grimshaw recently, so they took him instead. Damned nonsense all this talk, what? Feller's been dead nigh on a hundred years—why should he suddenly have people talking about him, and jump in value? Some sillyarse in Bond Street got it up, I suppose. Still . . .'

'Thirty thousand, he said, didn't he?'

'That's what I got him to. I think we should. Apparently the fad is getting to its peak at the moment, so Edwina said. We'd feel damned fools if we refused thirty for it now, then in a year's time it's only worth five again.'

'I can see that, Wooffy,' said his wife. 'Still, I'm not so sure. You've got to remember how well the house is doing. And the Grimshaw is one of the attractions. If that goes, there isn't anything very interesting in the picture line.'

Wooffy looked at her, affronted.

'Good heavens, woman,' he spluttered, touched to the quick. 'What arrant nonsense! There's Bootle's picture of m'grandmother! And what about the genuine Wither-spoon?'

HAPPY RELEASE

'Shall I freeze the rest of the stew, dear?' asked Herbert Greenaway, gazing almost amorously at the remains of dinner.

'Of course,' snapped Mabel Greenaway. 'You don't think I want to eat it again tomorrow, do you?' She did not bother to look up from her knitting. Knitting for Mabel Greenaway was a kind of tribal violence, with spears. It demanded concentration.

So Herbert Greenaway got from the kitchen cupboard one of the little tinfoil containers, and began spooning into it the remains of the evening's casserole. Good, domesticated Herbert.

In fact, good, domesticated Herbert did more than that. He added to the mixture one little mushroom before he finally placed the box neatly in the deep-freeze compartment which sat on top of the refrigerator. Quite an innocent-looking mushroom, especially after he had cut it up and disguised its odder features. But it was this mushroom that extensive reading, and his naturalist friend Fred Prior, had taught him was the most deadly growing in the British Isles.

Herbert came back into the sitting-room.

'I think I've got everything packed, dear,' he said.

Mabel sighed, gave one more venemous jab to the dead body of her knitting, and put it aside.

'You won't have. You're a perfect fool when it comes to packing. I'll have to go through it as usual. It's bad enough being left for two weeks, without having to nursemaid you before you go. But there, it's always the same . . .'

For Herbert was off to the Continent, on a business trip for the firm. Or so Mabel thought. So his firm thought.

In fact—Herbert smiled in voracious anticipation as he heard Mabel's heavy form heaving itself up the stairs

(Herbert had always liked big women, but enough had been enough many years ago as far as Mabel was concerned) —he was running away. With a secretary. Not with *his* secretary. That would have been vulgar. And inconsiderate to the Firm, to have one whole department disappear overnight. Actually he was running away with George Mason (of Business Accounts)'s secretary. With large-busted, wide-hipped, five foot nine Marcia Lemon—blonde, mascaraed, pneumatic Marcia. Herbert Greenaway flicked his tongue round his lips like a lecherous lizard, in anticipation.

She had arranged most of it. The false passports, the new identities, the money . . . all that money . . . the Firm's money (always a *mean* firm, Herbert felt, so it really served them right). He and Marcia would disappear without trace. Leaving behind . . . Herbert regarded the mushroom, gratuitous as it was, as the last deed of self-assertion of a disappearing persona; one final paying-off of scores before he became, in resurrection, a New Man.

And it would sit there, in the freezer, waiting until Mabel's salivary juices were tickled by the thought of a nice stew, with none of the bother of preparation.

'You'll want sandwiches,' said Mabel next morning. When he whimpered in protest she snapped: 'Of course you will. You're not paying the prices they charge for meals on those Channel ferries.'

She might have spoken more pleasantly. She felt quite friendlily disposed towards him. But she thought so sudden a change of demeanour might arouse suspicion in the man she intended to murder.

She cut, skilfully, thin slices of brown bread, and took from the refrigerator the tin of crab paste she had so carefully doctored the day before to simulate food poisoning in those so unfortunate as to eat it. For Mabel had worked all her life in a hospital dispensary, and had learned all there was to know about poisons. She had a sharp, inquiring mind that had hardly been stretched at all by her home life, and the marital companionship of Herbert Greenaway.

That'll teach him to go off on trips with his fancy woman! she thought. For she had found various tell-tale marks and odours on his clothes, had put two and two together, and made three and a half.

She buttered the bread and spread the crab paste thickly, thickly, between the slices. Considerate, thoughtful Mabel Greenaway!

'Well!' said Herbert Greenaway, as the hire-car driven by him sped out of Dieppe. 'That all went well! A piece of cake! Couldn't have gone better!'

Beside him Marcia Lemon puffed out her bosom. 'I told you there was nothing to worry about,' she said.

Herbert's eyes strayed from the road, sideways and down at the bosom. It was indeed a superb bosom—mountainous, firm and rounded. Others, others in the office, said that it was a cold bosom. In fact the Firm joke about Miss Lemon was that her best assets were frozen. But Herbert didn't feel that way. His experience of sexual abandon had not been so extensive since his marriage that he was inclined to quarrel with his good fortune.

'Golly, I'm a lucky man!' he now said.

'And I'm a lucky girl,' said Marcia, with a sort of simper. But she said it not altogether convincingly. Because after all what was Herbert Greenaway but five foot six and a half of middle-aged nothing-very-much? Balding, pasty, with a moustache that would have been Crippenesque if it had grown more luxuriantly. Whereas she, Marcia . . . well, she was a girl who knew her own value, as well as the value of pretty much everything else.

'You organized things a treat,' said Herbert. 'The false passports, the car, the transfer of the money.'

'Did you sign the cheque?' asked Marcia.

Herbert patted his pocket.

'All ready here. Just waiting for one of us to go and collect. Seventy-five thousand. We'll be in Brussels tomorrow,' he sniggered. 'Seems funny to think we're going in the wrong direction.'

'I told you,' said Marcia, 'I want us to be completely untraceable. After Newhaven we didn't exist.'

'You're marvellous,' said Herbert fondly, lecherously. 'Feeling better? Tummy OK?'

For Marcia Lemon, who loved travel, was a bad traveller, suffering agonies of fear on planes and agonies of sickness on boats. The great motive behind her plan of escape, her new identity, was to find herself safely on that land mass which is the Continent with no reason ever to leave it to return to sea-girt Britain. With every reason, in fact, not to. So as she had heaved and vomited in the Ladies on the Channel ferry, as she had emptied herself, it seemed, of everything she had ever eaten, she had said to herself, over and over, as if telling a rosary, the words: 'Last time, last time, last time . . .'

Now she nodded.

'Fine,' she said. 'I'm all right as soon as I get on dry land.'

Herbert was feeling happier and happier the further he drove along the coastal roads of Northern France. Happier, and the more inclined to wonder at his luck. They were now not far from Normandy—where Marcia had once spent a holiday—and he was almost chuckling as he breathed the heady air of freedom.

'Yes, I'll say this,' he repeated, for the umpteenth time, 'you did a wonderful job. Everything worked like clockwork.'

'I'm known at the office,' said Marcia, 'for my powers of organization.'

'But the passports, the documents, the forged driving licence—*I* don't know how you managed it at all.'

'I have friends,' said Marcia.

'I bet you have. A girl like you's always going to have friends. That's what amazes me—'

'What does?'

'My luck. My fabulous luck. I can't believe it. What could make a girl like you fall for an ordinary chap like me?'

Your signature, you weedy oaf. Your necessary signature on documents authorizing the transfer of funds. Your signature on cheques. Your signature as Head of Accounts (Foreign). Marcia smiled down at him.

'I've always liked the mature type,' she said. 'Dependable. Someone I can rely on.'

'Little girl!' said Herbert fondly. 'Well, from now on, you just lean on me. You've done too much up to now.'

'You did your bit,' said Marcia generously. 'That time when they rang from Brussels about the transfer . . .'

'Oh, I knew they'd do that. So unusual a transaction. I had the story ready.' Herbert was inclined to boast. 'There was nothing to it, nothing at all. Feel like stopping to eat? Nice restaurant along the way? Good French *déjeuner*, eh?'

'No, we want to get on,' said Marcia. 'We don't want to leave any sort of trail.'

'You're marvellous!' said Herbert, and put his hand tenderly on her knee. Her handbag nearly fell to the floor, and she grabbed it like a flash.

'Throw it in the back,' advised Herbert. 'You don't want to keep clutching it.'

'I like to keep it with me,' said Marcia. 'It's got all my little things.'

Like a gun, for example. Not that she intended to fire from this gun. Still, a gun may always come in handy, in an emergency, if things don't go quite according to plan. And Marcia could use it too, accurately. She had trained. Marcia, the good secretary, prepared for all Eventualities.

Now they had left the low, flat countryside and were approaching the cliffs of the coast Marcia loved. Wild, dangerous country. She looked around her, remembering landmarks.

'Quite remote, isn't it?' remarked Herbert.

'That's what I want,' said Marcia. 'No trail. We'll zigzag back across France—through out-of-the-way places.'

'Still, I don't quite see the point,' said Herbert. 'They'll know we've been to Brussels, and when.'

'You're not the planner,' said Marcia. 'Darling.'

She kept her eyes on the surrounding landscape. This was her country. This was where the idea had first seized hold of her. They had had to come here. It was the only place, the place she had chosen. At last, not long before sunset, she said: 'There!'

'What, my little darling?'

'I'm hungry. It's all that throwing up. I'll have to have something. You've got that hamper.'

'You deserve something better than Mabel's bleeding sandwiches,' said Herbert fondly.

'We're miles from anywhere. Sandwiches will be fine. Pull in here and we'll have a picnic.'

They pulled off the road, and Marcia, still clutching her handbag, got out of the car and stretched.

'Isn't it lovely? Cliffs and sea and sky. We'll just sit down and have a bite, then move on.'

She walked to the edge and looked over. The cliff hung over the sea: nothing to be seen below but rolling waves, blue-grey tipped with white—inviting, dangerous. Marcia had an uncontrollable, almost erotic, feeling of power. She had no fear of heights, no fear of emptiness, no fear of anything.

'Don't go too near the edge, my lovely,' called Herbert Greenaway. He sat down fussily on the coarse grass, hoping it wasn't damp. Then he opened the little picnic basket his wife had insisted he bring. He inspected the contents.

'Well, there's plenty. Not like Mabel to make enough for two . . . All crab. Still, crab's always nice, isn't it? And there's a bit of cake for afters . . . I can't say much good about Mabel, but I will say this: she makes a lovely fruit cake.' He popped half a sandwich in his mouth, and then another. 'Come on, Marcia. You said you were hungry. You can't live off scenery, you know. Got to keep body and soul together!'

But Marcia had taken the heavy revolver out of her handbag, and—filled with the exaltation produced by sea and sunset and the prospect of great wealth—had come up quietly behind Herbert as he swallowed the crust of his sandwich and hit him quickly and hard on the back of the head. Herbert keeled over on to the picnic hamper. Obedient, eager-to-please Herbert! Putting the revolver neatly back into her handbag, Marcia bent over Herbert's senseless body, removed his wallet and checked its contents, then took the body in her arms, walked a few steps to the edge of the cliff, and threw it over.

Herbert did not die instantly. A strong breeze from the sea wafted his body in towards the cliff face, and a lone, obstinate tree, growing in chalky soil, broke his fall somewhat at the bottom. But the incoming tide was already lapping at the roots of the tree, and one way or another it wouldn't be long.

Marcia Lemon did not even look down to see. She was possessed with a feeling of limitless opportunity. She stood alone on the cliff edge like a Greek goddess, amoral, unchallengeable. The strain of the day—the demeaning, emptying sea-sickness, the Customs inspection, Herbert's company and fatuous conversation during the long car ride—all that had reached the logical, planned-for conclusion. The perfect secretary had planned the perfect crime. In Brussels there awaited her wealth; and after that a new identity, travel, fun, smart friends. The beauty of her future and the perfection of her planning coalesced in her mind and drove her to new heights of exaltation. She was no longer a busty office girl, standard figure of fun, butt of lip-licking jokes. She was the perfect criminal: she was superb; she was supreme; she was unbeatable.

Suddenly, incongruously, her stomach rumbled. She looked towards the hamper.

She was also hungry.

DEATH OF A SALESPERSON

It was the last thing you would have expected, Lottie used to say to her friends, and to anyone who would listen. Because Westbury was one of those 'nice' suburbs of London (or dreary, inward-looking and conformist, depending on your point of view), where you simply wouldn't expect to find anything unusual. And yet somehow there had collected together at the leafy end of Crompton Road a group of people who (in Lottie's words) were unconventional, experimental in their lifestyles, and capable of cocking a snook at the platitudes of bourgeois living with which they were surrounded.

'When you think,' Lottie would say, 'how the whole area is jam-packed with people in boring, traditional two-parent situations, it's practically a miracle—except of course that I don't *believe*—that there are a few people here who really believe in attempting alternative lifestyles. I tell you, I wake up every day and feel I'm at the dawn of something new and exciting!'

The people to whom Lottie said this smiled politely. Those more aware of social change said to themselves: 'Survivals from the 'sixties,' while others just murmured, 'Kooks.' When they spotted her thereafter they tended to give her a wide berth. It was possible to be free-flying, adventurous and experimental, and still be something of a bore.

Lottie's little circle at the leafy end of Crompton Road (where it turns into Acacia Drive and becomes pure stock-broker's Tudor) was close but not large. Its centre was probably Mike, who with his three teenage children occupied the whole of No. 74. His wife had decamped with an Australian, and sent the kids the occasional postcard of

Bondi Beach. Probably being married to a television technician with irregular hours had not been much fun. At any
rate, Mike kept open house, had the occasional woman-
friend in, and the children came and went as they liked—
luckily they were old enough for that. Mike was big and
bear-like, and on a Saturday night if he was home tended
to get genially tiddly on cheap red wine.

Pam and Judith had the first-floor flat at No. 72. They had
what Lottie described as a stable and caring relationship, as
did Nicholas and Jonathan, who had the ground-floor flat
of No. 75. Though whether Nicholas and Jonathan's relationship would have been quite so stable and caring if the
Aids scare had not put the fear of mortality into them Lottie
was not quite sure: she knew that both of them had flitted
around a bit in the past, and she had caught Nicholas
quite often looking wistfully at desirable young men. 'But,
goodness, it's not a crime to fancy someone, is it?' Lottie
said.

Cybella, in a room at the top of No. 77, was black.
Sometimes Lottie was sceptical about Cybella—not because
she was black, heavens above no, she thought that was
super!—but because she felt she was not really 'one of us'.
She suspected that what Cybella really wanted was a nice
house and a husband and kids—the whole middle-class
set-up. She had once heard her describe her friends (who
had been *awfully* kind to her) as 'a queer lot'. You'd think
minorities would stick together, wouldn't you? Lottie
thought. But she rather suspected that Cybella went around
with them so much because she enjoyed mothering Mike's
kids.

And then there was Lottie. Whether Lottie had slid into
non-conformity, or been catapulted into it by the breakdown
of her marriage, no one was quite sure. She had gone to a
course in Milton Keynes and had come back, in her own
words, 'a terrific feminist', but that was probably a symptom
rather than a cause of marital disharmony. She told her

friends she simply couldn't live any longer in that stifling atmosphere of male competiveness and male aggression, and quite soon she had got her husband out and had the whole of No. 73 to herself—she and her two little girls. She had got herself an excellent alimony arrangement, due to a lawyer friend, and now she also had a part-time job as typist at an advertising agency.

'Is that compromising with the system?' she would agonize from time to time. But then she would excuse herself, saying: 'What is a single parent to *do*, with all the odds stacked against her when it comes to getting an interesting and fulfilling job?'

So now she was trying to bring up her children in a warm, responsive and non-violent atmosphere. She was not lonely at all, she told people, because there was Mike and all her other friends. And quite often her brother Gabriel came to spend the weekend with her. Gabriel was with a Vedta-orientated commune in North Wales, but he came and stayed with Lottie whenever he had tickets for Covent Garden.

So that was the group: the Westbury Originals, as they sometimes called themselves. The story of how the group's loyalty and supportiveness was tested began at Mike's on a Friday—'black Friday', as Lottie called it ever afterwards.

They were all of them there, including Gabriel, who was up for *Così Fan Tutte* the next night. Cybella was helping Mike's youngest, Annetta, with her homework. Cybella rather overdid the mothering of Mike's children, Lottie sometimes thought, because Mike was a wonderful mother as well as father. All the rest had got involved in a wide-ranging discussion on the decline of CND. There was a big rally, or at least a medium-sized one, planned for the next weekend with the theme 'Whither the Peace Movement?' and they were getting in early. Thrashing the subject about made them quite heated. Judith in particular (she worked in a casting agency, a job with a good deal of power) could get very bossy when the subject was close to her heart. 'Where has the passion gone?' she kept demanding, looking round at them accusingly as if they were each personally responsible for the declining passion for peace. The children soon got bored, and drifted off upstairs to play with their computers. Some of the group disapproved of computers, thinking them anti-social and anti-worker, but they had to admit they kept the children quiet.

They were just getting on to the thorny topic of relations with Eastern bloc peace movements when the doorbell rang.

Mike raised his eyebrows in astonishment.

'Can't be anyone,' he said. 'We're all here.'

He was gone for a few minutes, and in his absence the argument began again. Judith was just beginning to get really aggressive, wagging her finger at Jonathan, who didn't take these matters of principle as seriously as he should, when Mike came back with a small, fair-haired little thing who he said had come to the door asking if he had a fifty-pence piece for the gas.

That was their first sight of Davina Stubbs.

Whether it was true (as she later said) that Lottie had a shiver of premonition as Davina came into the room it is impossible to say. Certainly Lottie looked at her critically. Davina was an awfully pretty girl, but she was pretty in a *Womans-Owny* kind of way which was definitely not the way of the Westbury Originals. There was a coolness about her —not just her clothes (straw-coloured frock, gauzy little scarf tucked in at the neck), but her whole manner, as if she thought she would find them all interesting, but wasn't yet sure whether she wished to be one of them. She was certainly over-made-up by their standards, and perhaps by most standards, but this was explained by her job: she worked in the cosmetics section of the David Lewis chain store. She was a salesperson.

Davina came from Hackney. When she had got the job

in Westbury she had actually regarded it as a step up the social ladder (several of the Originals laughed behind their hands at that!) She had also, in Hackney, never come across people quite like Mike and his friends, though her manner was designed to hide this fact.

'Come on in,' called Judith, genially hectoring. 'We're discussing Cruise missiles.'

'Solving the world's problems,' said Jonathan.

'No, really,' said Davina, rather attractively shy, some of them thought, 'I don't think I have very much to say about Cruise missiles. I just wanted a 50p. Mike doesn't seem to have one.'

Several eyes flickered at that. Mike already!

'Sit down, sit down,' said Mike, gesturing to the floor with his big, pullovered arm. 'Say your say or hold your peace, but join the mob. We're going to have chilli or something eventually.'

'Oh, are we?' said Cybella, and disappeared into the kitchen.

'What I don't like about the peace campaign,' said Gabriel, starting up the discussion again, 'is the way it isolates just that one aspect, at the expense of a holistic approach. Basically, getting rid of nuclear weapons is only part of the larger struggle to recreate a sane environment and a sane living-style.'

So Davina got a fair taste, that evening, of the Originals' concerns. She noted how Pam took Judith's hand to try to stop her losing her cool. She saw Jonathan imitating Judith behind her back, and her growing, angry consciousness of it. She noted Lottie's flailing style of debate, and Nicholas's quiet fastidiousness. And she saw that Mike—big, genial, tolerant Mike—was the hub or lynch-pin of the group.

After a time the discussion petered out. Mike's two elder boys arrived back from the swimming pool, Cybella brought in the chilli, everyone fetched themselves wine from the winebox on the sideboard, and then everyone began to tuck in and to become more human. Cybella had to go to work (she was a receptionist at the local Trust House hotel, and she was on the night shift), and soon Lottie announced she'd better take her 'littlies' home. Davina took the hint and left then. Lottie muttered to Mike that she was a common little thing, and Pam said she hadn't got an idea in her head about Cruise missiles.

None of them expected to see her again, except to pass the time of day in the street.

So Lottie was a bit surprised, over the next few weeks, to find Davina so often in and out of Mike's house. Lottie would drop in to borrow rice, or brown sugar, or wholemeal flour, and there Davina would be. Eventually she said to Pam: 'At last the penny's dropped. She saw Mike—you know how he comes and goes at all hours—found him attractive, and invented the 50p as an excuse. Why come next door, after all? There are at least five bedsitters and flats in her own house. And she went off quite happily without one. She's soft on Mike!'

Eventually Lottie conceived another suspicion. She thought that Davina watched her comings and goings from her window, and made sure she arrived at Mike's five or ten minutes later. 'As if Mike and I aren't the oldest of friends!' said Lottie: 'I've been in his bed in my time, and it's a bit ridiculous to start getting jealous of me now!' She added: 'She's practically a member of Mike's household, you know.'

And so she was. She cooked quite often for the family, displacing Cybella—though Cybella was such a busy girl that she seemed quite glad of the rest, and certainly showed no resentment. Davina took Annetta's clothes in hand, bought new socks for the boys, and on one occasion—a spectacular triumph, but bitter for the rest—actually got Mike into a suit to take her out to dinner.

They had been so accustomed to living in and out of each other's houses that this affected them all. They felt they could no longer call Mike's house their own. Naturally they discussed the new order, in as charitable a manner as each could muster. One day Nicholas and Jonathan were round at Lottie's, trying some clothes on Beth, her youngest (Nicholas designed clothes, in a small way) when he happened to mention that he was using Davina to model some things in a fashion parade he was putting on for the Westbury Toc H and their wives.

'She does it quite well,' he said. 'Moves well. Has a certain . . . air. Remote, somehow.'

'Oh, she's more than just a pretty face,' said Jonathan. 'Mind you, not *much* more . . .'

'As to her *mind*, the least said the better,' said Lottie. 'She's given no evidence of having a brain in her head.'

'Such a relief,' said Jonathan, 'after all the rest of you. It's nice at last to have someone around with whom one has something in common.'

Jonathan affected, on occasion, the pose of being The Man in the Street. It was a pose that didn't become him, Lottie thought, especially as most real Men in the Street would have died rather than acknowledge any affinity. What really marked Jonathan off from the rest (Lottie told anyone who would listen) was that he was not really a thinker. Where they cared passionately about this planet and its future, Jonathan was essentially frivolous, a mocker, a free agent.

Opinions on Davina were divided in Pam and Judith's household too. Lottie was round there one Saturday, having an impromptu lunch of Cornish Pasty and a glass of lager, and she became aware (as she later told the Superintendent) of *tension*—something she had never felt between them before. For some time she could not pin it down to anything specific, but the root of it became obvious when Davina's name came up.

'I wonder she doesn't just move in,' said Pam, merely toying with her food. 'She might just as well.'

'If I was her I wouldn't want the responsibility,' said Lottie. 'By her account she's only twenty-one herself.'

'But it rather depends on what she's after,' said Pam.

'Perhaps she's not *after* anything,' said Judith.

It was said magisterially. The other two cast a covert glance at each other, and remained silent. It was Judith who spoke next.

'She strikes me as totally fresh, quite without guile,' she said.

Pam gave a bitter little laugh.

'On the other hand, Mike *is* in television,' Lottie said.

'Quite,' snapped Pam. 'And Nicholas is in clothes. I'm in radio, but she can't cultivate both Judith and me, and Judith is the better bet. So there's three members of the Originals worth cultivating, if you're a schoolgirl with ambitions. And does she cultivate them! If she finds Mike's clout as a technician doesn't get her far, she'll turn the full glare of her ambitions on to someone else.'

Pam's eyes swerved sideways to Judith. Judith had been looking stonily ahead of her, with an expression that could only be described as mulish. It was obvious she was smitten.

'In point of fact,' said Lottie, 'I'm not sure her ambitions are theatrical at all . . .'

Lottie heard Cybella's reactions to the new order when she met her coming out of the hotel where she worked, at the end of a shift.

'Long time no see,' Lottie greeted her.

'That's right. I just don't seem to have the time. And Mike's kids don't need me now. They've got Davina.'

'She hasn't quite moved in,' Lottie protested.

'Still, she's around if they need anything.'

'Mike's an awfully good parent *any*way,' Lottie said.

'Oh sure. Still, he tends to forget things, and he's at his job all hours. Davina is a good backstop.'

'You're just too *nice*,' muttered Lottie.

Really, Lottie meditated, you'd think Cybella would take her dislodgement from Mike's household harder than that. Didn't she see that Davina had designs?

Life in the group, at this point, went on pretty much as normal. They were in and out of each other's houses, they lobbied for this cause or that, they sat on the floor with fork meals and put the world to rights. They still went to Mike's house, though Lottie for one felt less free there, and none of them, naturally, brought up the subject of Davina there, even if she did not happen to be present. When she was there she sat with them quietly, apparently listening to the talk, whether it was of Peace, the environment, true Socialism, or the next step forward for women. Occasionally she would go with one or other of them to a meeting—a peace meeting with Judith, a feminist meeting with Pam, or to Mike's splinter Trotskyite group, which she openly laughed at afterwards. She also laughed when Nicholas gave her a cod invitation to a 'More Gays in Local Government' meeting. She soon lost her shyness, and began contributing to the discussions—in a very negative, reductive and anti-idealistic way, Lottie thought. She was horrified when Gabriel—up for the weekend to see *I Capuleti e i Montecchi* —actually described her as an intelligent girl.

'Intelligent?' Lottie said, louder than was necessary. Gabriel, who was very involved with himself, and the environment, did not catch the warning note.

'Yes. Awfully bright. And nice too. You're lucky to have her around.'

Another one who's been taken in, Lottie thought.

It was a day or two after this conversation that there was a further incident that made Lottie see that there were great changes coming in her world. She had gone over to Mike's, Beth clinging to one hand, Eve to the other. But when she pushed Mike's front door she found it was locked. She stood staring in disbelief. Mike's door was *never* locked in the evening! There was always someone around then, and Mike said that to lock it was so bourgeois and property-conscious. But now she actually had to ring the doorbell.

'Hello,' said Davina, smiling very sweetly, but standing plumb in the doorway.

'It was locked,' said Lottie, starting in.

'That's right,' said Davina, not moving. 'Mike's busy.'

'Busy?'

'Yes. He's got a shooting schedule to organize, and it's proving a bit of a problem.'

And since she actually went on standing there, Lottie had to turn round and go away. She was boiling. The incident summed up (she told Pam, to whom she resorted in her outrage) the difference one person could make to a group —even a happy, caring, fruitfully inter-relating group like theirs.

'Of course I realize it's only a matter of time before she moves in,' she concluded.

And she was quite right. However, the announcement of it took a form rather different from what she had expected.

They were all at Mike's except Gabriel, who was back at his commune. They were having a good evening, planning a big protest against the Channel Tunnel. Mike had sent his eldest out for pizzas from the Italian takeaway (they were using the various takeaways in the area more often these days, since Cybella was around less often), and everything was going with a swing until the pizzas had been cut up, and they had all collected glasses and gone along to the statutory winebox on the sideboard.

'Wait!' said Mike. 'We're having something special to-night. Fetch the champagne, Davina.'

It's coming, Lottie thought. She said:

'Champagne with pizzas?'

Three bottles of it, ready chilled in the 'fridge. Davina put them on the sideboard, and began getting out the cut-glass hock glasses.

'The fact is, we've got a bit of an announcement to make.'

Mike grinned at them—his most charming grin. 'You've probably guessed it already, but here goes: Davina and I are going to be married.'

Everyone but Lottie gave an amused groan.

'I hope you mean shacked up,' said Jonathan.

'Well, actually no,' Mike admitted. 'We mean married.'

That really shocked some of them.

'But you can't!' Lottie wailed. 'After all you've said about marriage as a male-instituted vehicle for female slavery! We've all been agreed about that—always. And what about your own experience of it? You can't, Mike. It would be a travesty of all you've ever believed in! It would be a betrayal!'

'It will be a registry office do,' said Mike, but hardly shamefaced.

'You might as well have gone the whole hog and hired St Margaret's, Westminster,' said Judith scornfully.

'Davina wanted a proper ceremony,' said Mike, still good-humoured.

'Oh, we never doubted who was behind it,' said Lottie. 'After all this pretence of being one of us—to entrap you into *marriage*!'

'I do agree with a lot of your ideas,' protested Davina. 'Quite a lot of them. But if we're going to live together, I want us to go into it intending it to be for good. You've got to face it, my generation sees things differently from yours. We're just not as radical as you were.'

Outraged middle-aged faces stared at her, pop-eyed. They had been put in the past tense!

'What poisonous rubbish!' Lottie said. 'Of course young people are radical. That's why we feel so close to them—we've retained our ideals.'

Davina shook her head. Marriage was making her determined.

'You're wrong. Young people have seen through a lot of your ideas. I think you just haven't noticed.'

'She's right,' said Terry, Mike's eldest, who hardly ever spoke when they were all round there. 'You're still living back in the 'sixties, you lot. It's pathetic.'

The way he said it, he could have been talking about the eighteen-sixties. It hit them like a wet towel. Tears of mortification stung Lottie's eyes, and she sat silent for several minutes. When she began to recover her self-possession, she was struck a second blow: the others seemed to have come round. Even Judith (who perhaps had never had any very serious hopes of getting an act together with Davina) was being rather jolly, and before long they were all laughing and chaffing and drinking toasts to Benedick the married man.

Lottie tried to drink, but she couldn't get a sip down.

'I'm sorry, it'd choke me,' she said, and walked from the room. She did not extinguish the merriment. As she shut the front door she heard laughter from the sitting-room. Well, at least she'd made it clear that she was one person who wouldn't compromise her principles.

It was six days later that Lottie heard Davina was dead. She met Cybella in the late afternoon in the greengrocer's, Lottie clutching her courgettes and Cybella looking terribly upset.

'Have you heard?'

'No. Heard what?'

'Davina's dead. Died this morning.'

Lottie was overcome. She sat down on a packing case outside the greengrocer's, her head swimming.

'It's horrible. I'm not going to pretend I liked her, but a young life like hers . . . You shouldn't have broken it like that.'

'Sorry. I thought you'd have known.'

'I haven't been . . . going around much these last few days. How did it happen?'

'They were on their way to see the vicar of St Matthew's. You knew Davina had persuaded Mike to have a church wedding after all?'

'She hadn't!' Lottie's outrage was such that she almost
seemed to suggest that Davina was well punished.

'She had—if it was possible, Mike being divorced, and
all that. They were on their way to have this talk with the
vicar, and as they went up the drive Davina took out her
mouth-spray—you know what she was like about personal
freshness—and as soon as she sprayed it in, she gagged and
said "ugh", and by the time Mike was ringing the doorbell
of the vicarage she was vomiting. She died a few minutes
later in the vicar's study.'

'Good Lord! But how on earth—?'

'I just don't know. But they've called the police in.'

Lottie's first thought was: now, if ever, we ought to be
supportive as a group. She hurried over to Mike's, but she
was met by Terry in the hall, and he said his dad was too
upset to see anyone. He'd been with the police all afternoon,
and now he was up in his room, still in a state of shock.

'Does anyone know how it happened?' Lottie asked.

'Cyanide in the mouth-spray,' said Terry, but Lottie
could get nothing more out of him.

That, at any rate, was something to pass on. Though the
Originals had been a bit splintered since the announcement
of the engagement—or at least Lottie had been splintered
off from the rest—now everything would be back to normal.
However, Lottie found that Nicholas and Jonathan were on
their way out to a gay disco (which was a bit *too* 'life must
go on', she thought), and Pam came to the door and said
that Judith was just too bowled over to talk about it. So in
the end Lottie had to go back home and thrash it out with
Gabriel (up for *Ballo in Maschera*), who of course knew
nothing beyond what she could tell him.

More facts emerged over the next day or two. The mouth-
spray had been in Davina's bathroom for two or three weeks,
and she had not used it because she had another in her
handbag. When this was used up, she replaced it with
the new one. Lottie had often commented on Davina's

finickiness, how aware she was of the impression she made on others, on her spraying herself here and there all the time. 'I'd never have called attention to it, if I'd realized,' she said now.

The spray, apparently, was a perfectly simple one, and it had a screw top, so probably anyone could have interfered with it. At least, anyone with access to Davina's flatlet.

'And that means us,' said Nicholas to Lottie, when they met in the street two days after Davina's death.

'Oh come: it could be anyone. She had family.'

'A mother, crippled with arthritis. Davina went to visit *her*, not vice versa.'

'Friends . . .'

'We were her friends. She didn't have any others that she was on visiting terms with. She'd just moved into the district, remember.'

'I do think you're talking nonsense,' Lottie said firmly. 'I'm just *not* going to believe it has anything to do with any of us. We're all dedicated to non-violence.'

'I'd love to see you telling that to the police,' said Nicholas. 'I can just see the expressions on their faces.'

And, to her surprise, Lottie found that the police did want to interview her. In fact, they talked to all the Westbury Originals in turn, because they quite soon found out from the young man in the bed-sit over the landing to Davina that they were the only people likely to have had access to Davina's flatlet. Lottie had in fact only been to Davina's once, and she told Jonathan she bitterly regretted it, though as Jonathan said, the police would probably say she'd have had access to her handbag, and thus to the spray, whether she'd been to the flat or not.

'Not if she'd only just put the new spray in,' said Lottie. 'I hadn't seen her for *days*. Then I'd have been free of all this murk, and suspicion, and nastiness . . .'

Lottie found it a funny feeling, talking to the police. She'd always been instinctively anti, of course, 'knowing how rape victims suffer at their hands,' as she said to Pam, 'not to mention anti-nuclear protesters, and anyone really *caring* in our society.' She had to admit afterwards that the particular policeman who interviewed her was not actually violent, but she said she could feel violence in the atmosphere.

The Superintendent, whose name was Sutcliffe, took her briskly through the background—no doubt it was the briskness that gave Lottie the feeling of violence in the atmosphere. He showed signs of irritation when Lottie tried to elaborate on what a wonderful, mutually supportive collection of people they were, but she managed to make the point nevertheless.

'We're just a tremendously close, caring lot of men and women,' she concluded.

'I see. But Miss Stubbs was quite a new member of the group, wasn't she?'

'That's right. She only moved here five or six weeks ago.'

'But you were all close and caring towards her? She fitted in well?'

'Wonderfully well.'

Lottie felt a tiny twinge when she said that. But how could she hurt Mike by making public what she really thought of Davina? And how could she bring the Originals further under suspicion by making clear to the policeman what they felt? The trouble was, Sutcliffe's scepticism, which had previously sailed over Lottie's head, now became more pronounced.

'Miss Stubbs was a shop assistant,' he said carefully.

'That's right. A salesperson.'

'Most of you are in rather more exciting occupations.'

'More creative, certainly.'

'And yet she was part of your group—'

'We're not *snobs*!'

'—and you were all of you in and out of each other's homes?'

'*She* was always in and out of Mike's!' This came out fast, and Lottie felt at once that it gave the wrong impression. She added: 'But of course you know why that was. Actually, I can't recall her ever being in my house, and I was only once in hers.'

'And when was that?'

'Oh, about ten days ago, I suppose. To return a book. It was just before she and Mike announced their engagement.'

'But the others may have been there more often?'

'Possibly. You'd have to ask. Davina was modelling now and then for Nicholas, so he probably went there to try things on her—*with* Jonathan, most likely. Judith may well have been there a fair bit, but Pam was *most* unlikely to have. Gabriel was never there, so far as I know. Cybella seemed to like her, so I should think she dropped in from time to time.'

'Thank you,' said Superintendent Sutcliffe, pondering. 'That tells me quite a lot. I take it, from what you say, that Judith was attracted to her, Nicholas found her useful, Cybella liked her as a person, while you and Pam were dubious or downright hostile.'

'No, really, that's not true—'

'Now let's come to this engagement. Did it set the cat among the pigeons?'

Lottie was annoyed. She felt rushed, confused and wondered whether she was making the right impression.

'Well, I mean an en*gage*ment. We're all *madly* against marriage—Mike as much as anyone, until then. We have no time for the dominance-submission pattern it implies. So we all—the rest of us, that is—did think it sad for Mike to dwindle into marriage. Of course, if they'd just been sleeping together, that would have been another matter.'

'I see . . . Do you think that the marriage may have been the catalyst behind this?'

'Certainly not!' protested Lottie. 'Absolutely unthinkable. It's nonsense to imagine anyone else could be involved—I mean, any of us. The thing must have been poisoned before she brought it home, that's what I think. Have you thought of the other salespersons in David Lewis's?'

'Yes, we have. Unfortunately your theory hits a snag. This mouth-spray is called *Autumnfresh*, and it's not yet on general sale. The head of the cosmetics section had three samples sent her, and she kept one for herself and gave out two to two of the . . . salespersons, just before the store closed for the day. Davina was one, and she remembers her putting hers straight into her handbag and going off with it. We've inspected the other two sprays, and they're perfectly innocuous. Since the head of the cosmetics section was very friendly with Davina, and thought her an excellent salesperson, we have no reason to suspect her.'

'I see,' said Lottie, digesting this information.

'Now, about this engagement . . .'

And off they went again. It soon became apparent to Lottie, rather to her chagrin, that he not only knew more than he had let on, but in some respects he knew a lot more than she did. He knew that Gabriel had taken Davina to *I Capuleti*, and had gone home with her afterwards. That shocked Lottie, and she had to bite back the opinion that the experience would have been wasted on one of Davina's intelligence. Sutcliffe knew that Judith had been a fairly frequent visitor to Davina's flat when Mike was working— though he also mentioned Judith's claim that 'nothing had happened'. He asked if Lottie thought that Pam would have been jealous, and Lottie said she was sure Pam would have been quite happy about it, or at any rate that she would have been 'civilized.'

'Well, anyway,' Sutcliffe said, in his dry, policeman's way, 'it doesn't seem likely that there was anything between Davina and Nicholas or Jonathan.'

'Nothing *sexual*, you mean,' said Lottie.

'Quite.'

'Because there *are* other things,' said Lottie, feeling she had scored a point.

The pattern of the next few days was made by the police interviews. One after another of the Originals went to the Station, and in the course of the questioning the police usually let slip—or dropped deliberately—some new piece of information about their investigations, so that gradually the group got a near-complete picture of what had happened. They had to chew it over together, and as it didn't seem right to congregate at Mike's as they had used to, they straggled one after another to Lottie's. She had got two quiches from the wholefood shop, and lots of salad stuff. Even Mike came, though he looked awful and was sadly quiet, Lottie squeezed his hand when she let him in, and though Lottie and Cybella were backwards and forwards to the kitchen, throwing salads together and opening bottles of Bulgarian Cabernet Sauvignon, they got the gist of things as the subject was tossed backwards and forwards.

'The police have changed their minds about the spray,' said Jonathan. 'They say the thing hadn't been tampered with.'

'Hadn't been tampered with?' said Gabriel (who was again at Lottie's, drawn irresistibly by the sensation). 'That sounds like the girl who hadn't been interfered with even though she'd been battered to death with a crowbar. Even I don't think the products of our consumer society are as deadly as *that*. Of course it had been tampered with.'

'Sorry. What I mean,' explained Jonathan, 'was that the spray container itself was completely as it left the makers'. The screw top had never been removed and put back. They think the concentrated potassium cyanide was injected down the nozzle of the spray.'

'How interesting,' said Gabriel. 'That would take time.'

'It would. Which rather rules out someone who made a thirty-second trip to Davina's loo.'

'What about the other two girls at David Lewis's?' asked Pam. 'Surely they could have injected the stuff into theirs at home, then switched it with the one in Davina's handbag?'

'Surely. But the problem is that the police are pretty sure it never *was* in Davina's handbag until the day she died. She had a mouthspray she was finishing up first. The boy in the flat opposite hers was only at Davina's once, and that was the day she was given the sample. He saw it on the bathroom shelf then. Pam says she saw it there on Friday —the day before she died. So neither of the girls she worked with could have done a switch easily. And none of us could, because we had no access to Autumnfresh. Hence, so the fuzz think, it must be one of us who holed himself up in Davina's bathroom for quite a while.'

Seated now with her salad and wine, Lottie shifted uneasily. It had occurred to her that the one who was most likely to feel sufficiently at home in Davina's bathroom to do that was Mike. She hoped no one else would think of that.

'Who had actually been in Davina's flat?' Cybella asked.

'All of us, apparently,' said Judith.

'Who had been since the announcement of the engagement?'

'All of us except Lottie,' said Jonathan.

'I was only in the flat once,' said Lottie. 'You were there, Nicky. It was about two days before the engagement.'

'That's right. You did go to the loo, but you were in and out. *Not* long enough.'

'Actually,' said Gabriel, 'I hadn't been there either, not since the engagement. We went to the opera together weeks before.'

'Right,' said Jonathan. 'Two out. The rest of us all had. I was there with Nicky two or three times, trying on clothes. Both of us were in and out of the loo—to wash hands, quite apart from anything else. Voilà us!'

He looked around, as if expecting the rest to come clean.

'I was there once after the engagement, to congratulate her,' said Cybella. 'To tell you the truth, I've no idea whether I went to the loo or not. It's not the sort of thing one notes down in one's diary.'

'I was there several times,' said Judith. 'I expect I went to the bathroom.'

'I went once,' said Pam. 'I was . . . happier about her after the engagement. I went to wish her well. I didn't go into the bathroom, but you've only my word for that. There was no one else in the flat.'

Really, thought Lottie, looked at objectively Pam is a very likely suspect. The woman scorned. I imagine the police have only her word that it was *after* the engagement she visited the flat.

'I went often, of course,' said Mike abruptly. 'I must have gone to the loo, on one or other occasion.'

'You don't need to explain yourself, Mike,' said Lottie warmly. 'you're one who isn't under suspicion.'

She looked around for the rest to back her up. She found they were all looking at their plates.

'Well, that didn't seem to get us very far,' said Gabriel. 'Perhaps we ought to look at motive.'

Here there was an uneasy shuffling of feet. This was something they all found far from easy to discuss in the presence of Mike.

'Right, darlings,' said Nicholas, 'this is going to be embarrassing, but the only thing to do is to be quite open about it. We'll examine every possibility, however far-fetched. Where shall we start? Let's say Judith. Now, Judith, you fancied Davina, right?'

Judith nodded, with some dignity. Lottie thought: But you could say that Judith had a better motive than Pam, after the engagement. I suppose that's what Nicholas will fix on.

'So Judith could well regard the engagement to Mike as a spurning of her advances. She could conceive a hatred for the poor girl, regard herself as having been used, or played with. I'm not saying you *did*, darling, merely that you *could have*.'

'Of course,' said Judith.

'And then there's Pam: as we could all see, she was madly jealous.'

'A bit jealous,' put in Pam, 'not madly.'

'However that may be, the engagement *lessens* the motive rather than the reverse. Still, you could have tampered with the thing *before* the engagement.'

'I was only in the flat *after* it,' said Pam.

'Point taken. But we only have your word for that.' Nicholas is quick, thought Lottie. The police are sure to check on that. 'Then there's Gabriel. He could have fancied her.'

'I did fancy her.'

Lottie tried to hide her look of contempt at her brother.

'Motive obvious: scorned advances. Jonathan and I are different. If Jonathan were the least bit bisexual—'

'But you know I'm not, my dears. Otherwise Cybella would certainly have been the object of my lustful advances.'

'What I've missed,' said Cybella.

'If he were, or if I were, there might lie a motive. Or do we fancy Mike, do you think? No, I think we'll have to come up with something non-sexual, and I'm open to suggestions.'

He looked around, but nobody, not even Lottie, could come up with any.

'Ah well, leave that open. Now, since we're on the subject of fancying Mike, both Cybella and Lottie fancied Mike, as we all know.'

'You can't know anything of the kind,' Lottie protested.

'I love him like a daughter,' said Cybella. 'You seem to forget how much *younger* I am than all of you.'

'Don't rub it in, darling. Ageism is quite as bad as racism, and some of us are sensitive. Anyway, who's to say you haven't got a father fixation? Why else hang around with all us pathetic oldies? And then you see the daughter-role taken over by someone else. And then there's Mike: he may have repented of his proposal—'

'I never did,' said Mike bleakly.

'Mike's not in question,' said Lottie.

'Oh, but he is. He may have felt he was being led by the nose, a Trotskyite lamb to the Christian altar. We all know what loss of one's Socialist purity means to someone like Mike. And then there's Mike's children.'

'Bring me in by all means, but leave them out,' said Mike. 'They all loved her. And can you really imagine them getting hold of cyanide?'

'What kids get hold of always surprises their parents,' said Nicky. 'Well, if we are to judge things so far, I'd say Pam was fairly strong on motive, but weak on opportunity, and the same goes for Judith and Cybella. I'd count Gabriel and Lottie pretty strong on motive, but weak on opportunity. I think Jonathan and I are weak on motive, but very strong on opportunity. I'd count Mike—well, I don't know how I'd estimate Mike from the point of view of motive. We just don't have the information.'

To take the heat off Mike, Lottie said: 'The idea that Mike might kill his own fiancée is about as farfetched as the idea that I was or am in love with him.'

To her amazement there was a general laugh.

'Oh, come off it, Lottie,' Pam said. 'You can't expect us not to have noticed that you've been making sheep's eyes at him for the past three years.'

So much for female solidarity, Lottie thought, boiling.

'You have loved him with a love that has made his life a burden,' said Jonathan.

'Don't,' said Mike. 'I hate pointless cruelty.'

'I'm not so sure it is pointless,' said Nicholas.

'Of course it's pointless, since she hadn't been near Davina's flat since the engagement was announced. And you said yourself that the only time she was there, she was in and out of the bathroom in no time, far too fast to inject the spray.'

'True, true. Still, she has such a first-rate motive: so besottedly in love with you for years, and your occasional kindness only making things worse. It's no secret you told Davina to come over to yours every time she saw Lottie going there. In view of that splendid motive, perhaps we ought to look more closely at means. For example, could she have got a spray of *Autumnfresh* from one or other of Davina's workmates? She could be a friend of one of them.'

'I do not make a habit of being friendly with salespersons in chain stores,' said Lottie waspishly. 'I'm not being snobbish. I just don't find them as stimulating as you all seem to.'

'Anyway,' said Cybella, 'they've both still got their sprays.'

'Hmm. Is there a photographic laboratory at this advertising firm you work for?' asked Jonathan.

'Of course there is,' said Lottie. 'It's one of the most important parts of any advertising firm.'

'Possible source of potassium cyanide,' Jonathan murmured.

'This is ridiculous!' protested Lottie. 'It's turning into a kangaroo court! We should be looking into who *else*—outside the group—could have wanted to kill her.'

But she got no response. There was a silence in the room that amounted to an Atmosphere.

'I wondered how any of us could have got hold of potassium cyanide,' said Nicholas meditatively. 'That's the answer.'

'Oh, for God's sake,' said Lottie. 'Mike's a cameraperson.'

'But Mike doesn't have your motive,' said Nicholas. 'Because in spite of what I said, all of us could see he was terribly in love with her, and stayed that way. And if he hadn't—all he had to do was break it off. You had motive, access to poison . . .'

'But I didn't go near her flat after the engagement was announced,' said Lottie. 'So the whole discussion is pointless.'

'But is *when* you went so important?' asked Nicholas

thoughtfully. 'It was clear which way the wind was blowing. We all sensed it—though we may not have expected *marriage*. Most of us were happy, because we liked Davina. You didn't—and I bet you sensed the danger twice as quickly as anyone else, because you were directly involved. You'd been angling for Mike for years, and it was clear long before the actual engagement that you'd lost him to Davina. So even when you went to the flat, just before the announcement, you had a motive.'

'I think we should cut this short,' said Lottie, getting up and collecting plates and glasses, since Cybella—absorbed in the discussion—didn't seem inclined to do it. 'I couldn't have injected cyanide into the spray. You agreed yourself I was no time in the bathroom.'

She looked triumphantly round, and saw that everyone in the room looked miserable and uncertain. But suddenly Nicholas jumped to his feet and grabbed her by the arm.

'You could have substituted!' he shouted. 'You could have substituted a poisoned spray you'd prepared here!'

'Don't be silly,' said Lottie, shaking him off. 'How could I have got hold of *Autumnfresh*? All the sprays are accounted for.'

But he held on to her.

'Who else would the makers have sent advance samples to, apart from stores that might stock it?'

The answer came from Lottie's own brother, sitting miserably on the floor.

'Advertising agencies.'

'Who had the *Autumnfresh* account?' shouted Nicholas. 'Who? Was it your firm, Lottie?'

'I don't know, I don't know,' she screamed back. 'You're all hateful, out of your minds. How could I know she had the damned stuff in her bathroom? Am I really the sort of person who goes round comparing notes about mouth-sprays with people?'

It was a point. Nicholas let go of her arm. Lottie was

turning to go out of the room when Cybella said: 'When you went there, Lottie, you were returning a book, weren't you?'

'Yes, I was.'

'When did you borrow it?'

Lottie looked at Cybella in silence for some moments, and when she failed to outstare her she turned and marched into the kitchen. She put the plates on the table, and then rested her hands on it to get her breath back. I'm silly to be upset, she thought. It's just a game. Maybe next time we get together they'll play Get Cybella, or Get Judith. It's Davina, dividing us in death, as she did in life. To think this was a close, loving little community of people before she came along and spoiled everything!

She started up, as she heard the front door shut softly. Going back into the living-room she saw them all scuttling away. Perhaps they felt ashamed. They were going to Mike's! Mike would stamp on all this nonsense. Dear old Mike.

It was the betrayal that hurt most, Lottie wrote in the article she sent to *Spare Rib*. That was the feeling that was uppermost in her mind when the police car drew up outside her house next day. That and the feeling that they had gone against all their principles: they hadn't only suspected her, they had gone to the police with their suspicions! 'When I remember how often we discussed alternatives to punishment, and caring community action as a substitute for policing, the sense of betrayal is total.' Once they had voiced their suspicions it was inevitable (though Lottie did not dwell on this) that the police should go along to Capstone and Willis, find out about the advance trade samples of *Autumnfresh*, hear about the loss of potassium cyanide from the lab. When you think, Lottie lamented, of all her cheerful endeavours to cement them into a happy, mutually support-ive team!

It was characteristic of Lottie that she ended her article,

smuggled out of Holloway Prison, on an up-beat note. It took some time, she said, to adapt to a confinement situation. But she had begun to collect around her a really super group of concerned and caring women, and she was coming to understand that only in an isolated, all-female community, totally cut off from a male-dominated, consumer-oriented society could true freedom for women be attained. Fancy having to come to prison, she burbled on, in very much her old manner, to experience real Liberation!

MY LAST GIRLFRIEND

'That's my last girlfriend,' said Miles, when he caught Deborah looking at the framed snap on the side table.

They were together on Miles's specially roomy sofa, and neither of them had a stitch on, though Miles had managed to retain his Sagittarius charm. Already Deborah was talking in terms of moving in. She was somehow on top of him when she spotted the photograph, and she swivelled round to sit by his long legs and look at it.

'She looks nice,' she said, unrancorously. 'Sort of pleasant —smiling.'

Miles turned and looked, apparently unconcerned, at the picture of him in full boating rig, standing beside the smiling girl.

'Oh yes,' he said. 'She smiled all right.'

'Who took the snap?'

'My pater. And he's about sixty-five, so you can get *that* thought out of your head.'

'Oh, I didn't mean . . . What a funny thing to say. After all, you can smile at people without meaning *that*, can't you?'

Miles curled his very handsome lip.

'Can you? I don't know that *she* could. She smiled at people a good deal too much, as far as I was concerned.'

'I expect you imagined it. Anyway, you didn't own her.'

'No?'

There was silence for a moment. Miles was now at one end of the sofa, his knees drawn up under his chin. Deborah was squatting at the other end, still looking at the picture.

'No,' she said, in her best attempt at a decisive voice. 'Of course she's got a right to behave how she likes to other people.'

'Matter of opinion,' said Miles off-handedly. 'It was the *way* she smiled I objected to.'

'Don't be daft. A smile is a smile.'

'No, it's not. Most people have many different ways of smiling. Not her, though. First time I noticed it I saw her smile at some old newspaper-seller who'd sold her the *Evening News*. Who'd bother to smile at some smelly old git like that? Then I'd take her to some Stock Exchange function, and she'd smile when I introduced her to my boss.'

'Well?'

'*In exactly the same way.*'

'Well, why not? Shows she was friendly.'

'Friendly! . . . Then I'd catch her at the window there, looking at the sunset, and the silly bitch would have the same smile, exactly the same smile, on her face. Who the hell smiles at sunset on the Thames Valley?'

'She just liked sunsets, I suppose.'

'But what really got me, *really* got me, was when I realized that when I came down to breakfast in the morning, or when I got home at night, she'd smile at me—*me*—in exactly the same way.'

'What did you expect?'

'Something different! Something special! Something to show that I was *the* person in her life. Special. Was she my girl, or was she not? I didn't take up with her to be treated exactly the same as a bloody setting sun!'

'You could have told her. Talked it over with her.'

'I wouldn't stoop so low.'

'She looks awfully young. If you'd told her what was niggling you, you could have made her understand.'

'It would have come to an argument. I couldn't have had that. I never argue with people. If she didn't understand *naturally* what I had a right to expect, she'd never understand at all.'

'I think you're a pig. I suppose you got rid of her.'

'That is pre*cise*ly what I did.'

'Just threw her over.'

'Not exactly, though it's an idea. Let's just say that I stopped her smiles altogether.'

Deborah had been getting restless for some minutes. That last remark of Miles, said with a cat-like smile on his handsome face, made her sit in silence for some moments. Then she reached for her tights and bra.

'What did you mean, about stopping her smiles altogether?' she asked, in a voice that came out small and tight.

'Just what I said. I made sure she never smiled at me or anyone else like that again. Ever.'

'You don't mean you . . . *did* something to her?'

'I should be so stupid! I'd have been the first one they came for, wouldn't I? Still, something had to be done, that was for sure. I couldn't have her talking about me to other men . . . laughing at me . . .'

Deborah had her skirt on now, and was reaching for her blouse.

'What did you do?'

'I've got friends . . . I was at a gala concert at the Festival Hall that night. Then at the reception afterwards . . . But they're good friends. I'd do the same for them . . . For quite a small consideration they did what had to be done. There was nothing to connect them with her, you see. They'd never met her . . . It all went off very smoothly.'

'I don't believe this. This isn't happening.'

But she had got her handbag, and was turning to the chair where she had slung her coat. Miles shrugged, still with the same self-absorbed smile on his face.

'As you like,' he said.

'You wouldn't . . . have someone *killed* . . . just because they didn't give you the . . . *devotion* you wanted.'

'I can't think of a more terrible failure, in someone *I* had chosen.'

She was at the door. Bravely she turned and said:

'You'd have to be a *monster*.'

'Perhaps there is just a little element of the monster in me. But a frightfully handsome monster, don't you think? Why don't you come back, just for a while?'

Negligently, beautifully, he started up from the sofa. Deborah turned on her heels, wrenched open the door and fled, her high heels making a clap-clapping sound as she trundled herself down the stairs.

Miles lay back on the sofa, still smiling in self-contentment. An English degree at Oxford had been no sort of preparation for a career on the Stock Exchange, but he never regretted having been forced to read 'My Last Duchess'. It had been invaluable in getting rid of girlfriends who had started becoming proprietorial.

Lazily, still smiling, he leant round and turned the snapshot of his sister and himself, taken at Henley, face down on the side table.

He'd never liked his sister's silly smile.

FREE FROM DELL

with purchase plus postage and handling

Congratulations! You have just purchased one or more
titles featured in Dell's Mystery Promotion. Our goal is to
provide you with quality reading and entertainment, so we
are pleased to extend to you a limited offer to receive a
selected Dell mystery title(s) *free* (plus $1.00 postage and
handling per title) for each mystery title purchased. Please
read and follow all instructions carefully to avoid delays in
your order.

1) Fill in your name and address on the coupon printed below. No facsimiles or
copies of the coupon allowed.

2) The Dell Mystery books are the only books featured in Dell's Mystery
Promotion. No other Dell titles are eligible for this offer.

3) Enclose your original cash register receipt with the price of the book(s)
circled plus $1.00 **per book** for postage and handling, payable in check or
money order to: Dell Mystery Offer. Please do not send cash in the mail.
Canadian customers: Enclose your original cash register receipt with the
price of the book(s) circled plus $1.00 **per book** for postage and handling in
U.S. funds.

4) This offer is only in effect until April 29, 1991. Free Dell Mystery requests
postmarked after April 22, 1991 will not be honored, but your check for
postage and handling will be returned.

5) Please allow 6-8 weeks for processing. Void where taxed or prohibited.

Mail to: Dell Mystery Offer
P.O. Box 2081
Young America, MN 55399-2081

NAME_____

ADDRESS_____

CITY_____STATE_____ZIP_____

BOOKS PURCHASED AT_____

AGE_____

(Continued)

Book(s) purchased:_____

_____

_____

I understand I may choose one free book for each Dell Mystery book purchased (plus applicable postage and handling). Please send me the following:

(Write the number of copies of each title selected next to that title.)

☐ **BLOOD SHOT**
Sara Paretsky
V.I. Warshawski is back—this time a missing person assignment turns into a murder investigation that puts her more than knee-deep in a deadly mixture of big business corruption and chemical waste.

☐ **FIRE LAKE**
Jonathan Valin
In this Harry Stoner mystery, the Cincinnati private eye enters the seamy and dangerous world of drugs when a figure from his past involves him in a plot that forces him to come to terms with himself.

☐ **THE HIT MAN COMETH**
Robert J. Ray
When a professional hit man who has his sights set on a TV evangelist wounds Detective Branko's partner instead, Newport Beach's hottest detective finds himself with a list of suspects that is as bizarre as it is long.

☐ **THE NANTUCKET DIET MURDERS**
Virginia Rich
A handsome new diet doctor has won over Nantucket's richest widows with his weight-loss secrets—and very personal attention. But when murder becomes part of the menu, Mrs. Potter stirs the pot to come up with a clever culinary killer.

☐ **A NOVENA FOR MURDER**
Sister Carol Anne O'Marie
"Move over, Miss Marple, here comes supersleuth Sister Mary Helen, a nun with an unusual habit of solving murders."
—*San Francisco Sunday Examiner & Chronicle*

☐ **SHATTERED MOON**
Kate Green
When a young woman gets involved with the L.A.P.D. and a missing person case, her most precious gift—her healing vision—becomes her most dangerous enemy, filling every moment with mounting menace. . . and turning the secrets of her past murderously against her.

☐ **TOO CLOSE TO THE EDGE**
Susan Dunlap
Jill Smith, a street-smart, savvy detective, finds herself trapped within a murder victim's intricate network of perilous connections.

☐ **A NICE CLASS OF CORPSE**
Simon Brett
When the sixty-seven-year-old Mrs. Pargeter checks into a seaside hotel for some peace and quiet, what she finds instead is a corpse in the lobby and a murder to snoop into on the dark side of the upper crust.

☐ **POLITICAL SUICIDE**
Robert Barnard
A member of Parliament meets an untimely—and suspicious—demise.

☐ **THE OLD FOX DECEIV'D**
Martha Grimes
When the body of a mysterious woman is found murdered, Inspector Richard Jury of Scotland Yard finds himself tracking a very foxy killer.

☐ **DEATH OF A PERFECT MOTHER**
Robert Barnard
Everyone had a motive to kill her. . . so Chief Inspector Dominic McHale finds himself stumped on his very first homicide case—puzzled by a lengthy list of suspects and a very clever killer.

☐ **THE DIRTY DUCK**
Martha Grimes
In addition to the murders being staged nightly at the Royal Shakespeare Theatre, a real one has been committed not too far away, and the killer has left a fragment of Elizabethan verse behind as a clue.

TOTAL NUMBER OF FREE BOOKS SELECTED ____ X $1.00
= $_____ (Amount Enclosed)

Dell has other great books in print by these authors. If you enjoy them, check your local book outlets for other titles.